Ellie stared in confusion at the bedraggled man on her front porch. Had she forgotten about a guest's arrival?

Su ked.
Th tely
wit fled
aro

the
life man
bef lder
of tter
yet d at
her

drel
tha his
dea

PAIGE WINSHIP DOOLY enjoys living in the South with her family, after having grown up in the sometimes extremely cold Midwest. She is happily married to her high school sweetheart, Troy, and they have six homeschooled children.

Books by Paige Winship Dooly

HEARTSONG PRESENTS

HP84—Heart's Desire
HP775—Treasure in the Hills
HP807—The Greatest Find

Carousel Dreams

Paige Winship Dooly

Heartsong Presents

To Doug and Lyn W., my inspiration for the characters in this book. We love you!

A note from the Author:
I love to hear from my readers! You may correspond with me by writing:

Paige Winship Dooly
Author Relations
PO Box 721
Uhrichsville, OH 44683

ISBN 978-1-60260-100-0

CAROUSEL DREAMS

Our mission is to publish and distribute inspirational products offering exceptional value and biblical encouragement to the masses.

PRINTED IN THE U.S.A.

one

"Grandmother. . .these books can't possibly be correct. If they are. . ." The melodic feminine voice drifted off momentarily then resumed, stronger. "Did Papa keep another set of books somewhere? Maybe that would explain things."

The raised voices carried through the open window. Bascom's steps slowed on the walkway as he neared his destination—the large front porch of the resort. He'd just arrived in town and couldn't wait to see the owner's face when he presented the plan for his newest, hand-carved carousel. Of course, true to his reputation, he'd saved the most special pieces to carve once he arrived at the site. He never added his signature touches until he knew the personality of the owner.

"No, Ellie, he only kept one set of records."

This voice, decidedly older, contained more control, didn't sound as panicky. Bascom had to lean forward to hear. It wasn't that he wanted to eavesdrop, but he didn't feel comfortable intruding on someone during a personal discussion, either. He glanced around, weighing his options. There weren't any other buildings nearby, and his entire caravan of wagons that had followed him now waited to be unloaded. Bascom only needed to ask where to direct the drivers. He motioned for the nearest wagon master to wait a moment.

"Gram, what was Papa thinking? This can't be right. According to these numbers, Papa spent most of his fortune just before he died. How can that be?"

"Child, you can't question your grandfather's motives when he isn't here. It's not proper." The older voice didn't contain any of the worry the younger one portrayed. "Your grandfather had his reasons for everything he did."

"And his reason for this, do you know what it was?" Now the speaker spoke with venom. "It says here he purchased something. The paper is smudged, and I can't make out what it is."

A sigh carried through the air. "He purchased a carousel, Ellie. He wanted to surprise you."

Bascom heard the sound of papers shuffling.

"A carousel? For this outlandish amount? Why would Papa do this?" Despair crept into her words.

Bascom felt a pang of sympathy. He also felt a tug of panic. His works were usually embraced with enthusiasm. Never before had he approached a buyer who held such resentment. Yet his men waited to complete the delivery so they could be on their way to well-deserved breaks while he made the finishing touches and put the large structure together.

His apprentice, Sheldon Lavery, hopped down from the wagon and approached him. As usual, the man looked remarkably well-groomed with every dark hair in place, even after the long trip. "What seems to be the problem, boss?"

Bascom nodded toward the open window as the women resumed their discussion and put a finger to his lips to silence Sheldon.

"I suppose he thought the purchase would help us out."

"What would help me out would be to have that money in hand to help run this place." Footfalls sounded as the speaker paced. "I mean, really. His entire life's savings? How are we going to keep the resort afloat?"

Now guilt joined Bascom's sympathy and panic.

He heard Sheldon's snicker beside him. "This is grand. We

arrive with their carousel only to find out they don't want it."

Bascom silenced him with a glare. He didn't see any humor in the situation at all. His one-of-a-kind masterpiece had become his client's worst nightmare.

"Competition's fierce of late, Ellie. You of all people know that. Your grandfather knew we had to have an edge to keep the resort filled with guests. Amusements such as the carousel are the newest way to ensure such a thing."

Bascom could see silhouettes of the women through the window, though he couldn't clearly see their features. While the younger woman paced, the older one sat in her chair, some sort of needlework in her hands.

Sheldon leaned closer. "Are we just going to stand here and listen in on their conversation? Or are we going to alert them to our presence? Because. . .I don't think they're going to improve their image of us if they look out to see us cowering behind this rose trellis listening."

"What do you recommend I do, Mr. Lavery? The woman obviously had no clue this was in the works. She's financially strapped due to our gain. I'm trying to figure out a plan."

"Could we resell it to another client?"

Bascom shook his head. "It's doubtful. This one was pretty specific, and all our clients have their own minds when it comes to what they want to see designed for them. The odds are against someone else wanting a carousel of this nature."

"Then we seem to have no choice. The contract is sound. It's too late for them to back out."

If only it were so simple. Bascom didn't hurt for money, and these people obviously did, but he couldn't afford to write off or walk away from a project of this magnitude.

For the first time the older woman lowered her piecework. She tipped her head to stare over the top of her spectacles at her granddaughter. "The Lord always provides, dear. You know that better than anyone."

"Of course He does, but I believe He also expects us to use common sense when planning how to use what He's provided."

"Ellie Lyn, you know how your grandfather felt about you. You've always been his pride and joy. We've both sat back and watched the spark flow right out of your eyes. First when you lost your parents and later when you lost your sweet husband. The carousel purchase wasn't about the money. . . . It was your grandfather's way of making a smile reappear on your face. He felt concern for you, and this is what he wanted to do with *his* money." She paused as if to emphasize the point. "What's done is done, and I suggest you move forward with that fact and focus on the next thing. The contract has been signed, long ago, and the carousel is on its way. Like it or not, there's no changing that."

"Well, perhaps I can implore the builder to take it away and sell it somewhere else. Or I can refuse delivery. . ."

The grandmother's patience must have been spent, judging by the volume of her sigh. "And what good will refusing delivery bring? The money's already spent. It's gone. If you refuse delivery, you'll have nothing to show for your grandfather's well-intended decision."

"I guess you're right." The younger woman paced again from one side of the window to the other and momentarily disappeared from sight. "But I have to wonder what kind of dirty, rotten scoundrel takes advantage of an old man on his deathbed. Surely the builder knew of Papa's condition. Maybe we could hire an attorney, prove that the builder deceived or tricked Papa into this transaction."

Sheldon snickered again, and Bascom made his decision on the spot. It was one thing to regret a purchase of such magnitude, especially in this case without having any knowledge of the expense, but it was another thing altogether to stand there and insult his company and his name. He stalked up the stairs and knocked firmly on the door.

The voices instantly quieted. After a moment the door was yanked open, framing the most beautiful dark-haired, green-eyed beauty Bascom had ever seen.

ↄ•

Ellie stared in confusion at the bedraggled man on her front porch. Had she forgotten about a guest's arrival? Surely they didn't have anyone planned that she'd overlooked. Their rooms were full. But things had been rather chaotic lately with her papa's death and trying to get the resort shuffled around. "Can I help you?"

"Miss Ellie Lyn Weathers?" He looked perturbed, but for the life of her, she couldn't imagine why. She'd never seen the man before in her life. His unkempt brown hair brushed the shoulder of his jacket and looked in need of a good combing—or better yet, a nice visit to the barber. Confused blue eyes stared at her with consternation.

"I'm sorry. Do I know you?"

"I guess not. I'm Bascom Anthony, the dirty, rotten scoundrel that you think took advantage of your grandfather on his deathbed."

"Oh dear."

Her grandmother's soft laugh echoed from behind. " 'Oh dear' is right. Ellie Lyn, I've warned you that your quick tongue was going to catch you in a spot."

"Thanks, Gram, that really helps." Ellie now felt as exasperated with her grandmother as she did with the stranger standing on their threshold.

The man continued to stare, and Ellie didn't know what to do. Fortunately, her grandmother picked that moment to join her at the door and motioned the man inside. He removed his dusty hat and hung it on the rack that stood near the door.

He walked with a slight limp as he moved into the foyer.

"I apologize for my appearance. We've just arrived in town, and I came straight over."

"We?" Ellie leaned past and peered over the man's shoulder. She gasped when she saw all the men and wagons. Each wagon contained several large wood crates.

"Yes, we. I have a caravan of men that have helped me transport the attraction, and they're waiting for direction on where to unload. I'm sorry if we've caught you at a bad time, but they really need to be able to get on to their other destinations. They'll move on while my assistant and I do the finishing touches."

"But how big can this carousel possibly be?" Ellie's wayward curls had tumbled over her shoulder, and she brushed them back with frustration. "I thought it would be brought in and that would be that."

Bascom laughed. "It isn't that easy. I still have to put it all together. There are still a few pieces to carve and design. I'll be here awhile."

"And where will you stay?"

"According to my contract, I'm to stay here. Your grandfather was most specific. He wanted me to have full access to my work while putting the carousel in place."

Ellie's grandmother stepped forward. "I'm so sorry. We haven't even properly introduced ourselves. Let's start over. I'm Mary Case, and this is my granddaughter, Ellie Lyn."

"Pleased to meet you both."

Ellie muttered under her breath. "I'm sure."

"Excuse me?" The man appeared baffled. Surely he wasn't that daft.

"You can't possibly be pleased to meet us under these circumstances. If you overheard my comment about the wool being pulled over my grandfather's eyes—"

The man had the audacity to interrupt. "I believe the phrase you used was, 'dirty, rotten scoundrel.'"

"Right. I believe it was something like that. Though from outside I'm sure you couldn't hear clearly."

"Your words were loud and clear, ma'am."

"And for my words, I apologize." Ellie couldn't look him in the eye. "I'm sorry you overheard that conversation."

Bascom's mouth quirked up to one side, the action more grimace than smile. "So, you're sorry I overheard, but not as sorry for your words?"

"Well, you have to understand how it looks from my viewpoint..." Her voice trailed off as she caught her grandmother's scowl.

Grandmother pushed Ellie aside, none too gently, and ushered the man into the parlor. "Have a seat here and let me get you a cool drink. I'll send someone out to serve your men cool drinks as well while they wait."

She left Ellie alone with the stranger. He stared expectantly at her. She felt she owed him an explanation. "You see, my assistant, Wanda, and I had this dream. We thought we could compete with the bigger resorts if we offered a novelty, such as a carousel. We researched and decided the expense too great to justify for a resort of our stature. My grandfather must have overheard our plans and decided to take control of matters on his own." She wrung her hands together. "We lost him recently, and the last thing I anticipated was that he took everything he had and put it all into your creation. To say the least, the whole idea has caught me by surprise."

Bascom studied her. "Perhaps your grandfather felt it a final gift to show his love for you. He had faith you could use the attraction to the resort's best interest." He glanced toward the kitchen as Grandmother brought in his drink. "He confided in me and said as much. He didn't tell me he wouldn't be around to see his plan put into action. I am sorry for your loss."

Ellie felt shame over her words and attitude. "I do want to apologize. I really am sorry." She took a deep breath. "And we'll figure out a way to make things work so we can carry out my grandfather's final wish."

"I have the perfect solution." Gram didn't seem at all remorseful about her obvious eavesdropping. "Since the upstairs rooms are full, Ellie, you can move into Priscilla's room. She has a large bed, and you know she'll love the arrangement. Wanda can move into your room, and Bascom can use Wanda's room off the kitchen until his stay is up. With its private entrance to the porch, he'll have freedom to come and go without disrupting the household."

The plan could work. The family quarters were at the back of the house on the main level. Having a man around would be awkward to say the least, but it wouldn't really present a hardship. As her grandmother had said, he'd have privacy and so would they.

The kitchen door burst open, and Ellie's five-year-old daughter, Priscilla, flew into the room. "Mama, look! I made a snake!" A piece of dough dangled from her fingers, having been rolled into a snake's form during her table play while under Wanda's supervision.

Ellie feigned a shiver of disgust, which earned a giggle from the little girl.

"It's not real—it's pretend. Like the Land of Whimsy." Prissy froze and stared as she finally noticed her mother and grandmother weren't alone.

"Prissy, this is our newest guest, Mr. Anthony. He'll be staying with us for a while. He has a special project that will help the resort bring in more business." Or at least she hoped as much. Winter was always tough on Great Salt Lake, and this year had been no exception. Bigger hotels were moving in, and new attractions—such as the newly famous Saltair Resort—made the competition fierce.

Bascom smiled at Priscilla, a genuine gesture, complete with dimples that transformed his face.

"I'm glad to meet you, Priscilla." He glanced at Ellie. "Please tell me about the Land of Whimsy. It sounds most intriguing."

A warm flush moved up Ellie's face. "It's nothing really."

"It isn't nothing, Mama!" Prissy gasped with indignation. She turned to their guest, her eyes sparkling with enthusiasm and her voice lowered to a whisper of awe. "The Land of Whimsy is our special place. Mama tells me Whimsy tales every night before I go to bed. Whimsy is a place full of sea creatures and princesses and all sorts of exciting adventures."

"Is that so?" To his credit, Bascom really did seem intrigued, as if the information had been set aside for further thought. Though why he would care about Ellie's make-believe world was beyond her.

two

Ellie placed a pan of cookies onto a rack and slammed the oven door closed with too much force, an action that earned her a questioning glance from Wanda.

"I don't understand why you're so upset." Wanda dusted her flour-coated hands against her apron and began to knead the large ball of dough before her. Her robust form pressed against the countertop as she worked the lump into smaller circles that would soon become their dinner rolls. "This is our chance. We've dreamed of this opportunity for a long time, and thanks to your grandfather—rest his soul—we now get to see our carousel dreams come to life."

"It's. . .I don't know. The whole thing feels wrong." Ellie strode over to look out the open kitchen door. A gentle breeze blew in and cooled her overheated face. Her eyes were immediately drawn to the action near their largest outbuilding behind the resort. The men, *Bascom's* men, had lined up their wagons and worked as one to move each crate along a human chain before the wooden boxes disappeared into the carousel's new home. One wagon would be unloaded and the driver would move out of line and another would take its place. She shook her head. "Look out there! All those men are rushing around in such a hullabaloo of activity for such a silly notion. My grandfather should not have taken my fantasy to the point of fruition."

She folded her arms across her chest, leaned against the doorway, and watched. She started when she felt Wanda's gentle hand wrap around her arm.

"You're feeling guilty."

14

The comment took her by surprise. "Guilty? Why do you say that? I didn't order the contraption."

"No, but you wished for it, and you feel that your dream put the event into motion."

"And didn't it? Papa would never have thought up such an outlandish idea on his own. He carefully planned and plotted out every detail of his life." Her voice rose in agitation, regardless of her attempts to quell it. "And then he threw everything away to appease me. He wasted his life savings. We have nothing to show for his hard work, all his planning. . ."

"You just said yourself that your grandfather was a careful man. Do you really think he'd risk it all if he didn't have good reason? Maybe he knew you were onto something great and without a push you'd never take the necessary risk to reach that goal."

Ellie nibbled her lower lip and considered Wanda's words. Though only a few years older, Wanda always had wise advice. "Maybe."

"And the reality is—the attraction is here. Delivered by a very handsome man, I might add." She nudged Ellie and received a reluctant grin. "You have to admit Bascom is a nice bonus to the deal."

"I'll admit no such thing." At that moment Bascom glanced her way and waved. She quickly moved away from the door.

Wanda's quiet laugh followed her. "Then why did you just run away from his wave? The man is only being friendly."

Flustered, Ellie pulled open the oven to peer in at the under-cooked pastries. "I thought I smelled something burning."

"Perhaps it was your ears. They're burning red all the way to your hairline. And all because a man you don't find attractive sent you a good-natured wave." She tsked and moved back to her rolls.

"Can I help you with those?" Other than removing the last

of the cookies from the oven, Ellie's own chores were done. Though they had extra men to feed, they'd prepared a hearty beef-and-vegetable soup earlier in the day, so dinner would be easy. Wanda's crusty rolls and Ellie's snickerdoodle cookies would round the meal out nicely. The majority of their guests had taken advantage of the noisy evening to escape to nearby Saltair Resort for dinner.

"I only have to place them on the pan. You sit and relax while you have a chance. I'll join you in a moment."

Ellie did as advised and with a few minutes to spare watched her friend work. Even this late in the day Wanda as always looked as neat and fresh as she had upon rising early that morning. Every hairpin remained in place, holding Wanda's soft brown hair in check while Ellie's own dark curls fell out of her pins in tumultuous chaos. Though she repaired it several times a day, the outcome always remained the same.

The comparison made her feel like a wild filly next to Wanda, the pristine mare. If Bascom had any intent through his wave, it was probably to capture her shapely friend's attention. She sighed.

Wanda chose that moment to set a cup of tea before her. She sank into the opposite chair with a smile. "Talk to me. Why all the anxiety?"

Ellie's eyes returned to the activity outside their window. "I've worked hard these past two years since losing Wilson to his illness. Priscilla and I have made our own way, and we've succeeded." She realized she was scowling and forced herself to relax. "Bascom takes up a much-needed room here at the hotel."

"Your room wouldn't have been rented out, Ellie. Our shuffling around didn't change anything. And the carousel is new and unique and bringing in crowds at other hotels. I think this is a much needed move. Your grandfather didn't enter into his decision easily. He never did." A soft smile shaped her mouth. "And I think God handpicked Bascom to build it for us. I've seen the paperwork. He gave us a great price. You know that having a B. A. Carousel can only help with our future finances. People are buzzing over his work, and he's careful to only create one masterpiece per area. We're blessed to have been accepted as clients. When word gets out that we have an original, people will come to see it—people who wouldn't have come here otherwise. I can't wait to see the theme he's chosen."

"Theme?" Ellie wrinkled her forehead again. "I thought carousels were pretty standard. A few benches, moving horses of various color, and sometimes swans that rock back and forth."

Wanda's eyes lit with anticipation. "Bascom's carousels always have a theme, built around the personality of the person who orders them."

"But whatever would Papa's theme be?" Ellie couldn't imagine how her grandfather's life would be immortalized. "He worked hard. He rested in his rocker on the front porch in the evenings while smoking his pipe and visiting with the guests. I'm not sure that will make for a very exciting attraction."

"This is where the fun begins!" Wanda sent Ellie a pointed grin as she walked to the oven and removed the final tray of cookies. The scent of warm cinnamon and sugar drifted through the room. Wanda placed the pan on a cooling rack with the others before she replaced it in the oven with the two pans of rolls. "Bascom always gets to know the owner before finishing the final design. Since your grandfather is gone, you'll be the center of Bascom's plan."

Ellie felt a momentary panic. She didn't like being the center of anything, let alone the focal point of a stranger's plan. She felt like a specimen under the lens of a man who studied a scientific process.

"I'm more predictable than my grandfather. How will he ever come up with a theme about me? This carousel will be his first flop." Ellie did her best to stay out of the limelight. She buried her face in her hands. This latest information was disheartening.

Wanda's laugh surprised her. "Oh honey, why do you always underestimate yourself? If anything, he'll have to juggle ideas and choose which is best to encompass your personality into one small project such as this. You'll be his greatest endeavor, just you wait and see."

Ellie noticed the activity outside had slowed. "It looks like the men are down to the last wagon. They'll soon be ready to eat. I'd best go wake Prissy and Gram from their naps."

She shivered with dismay as she mulled over Wanda's words and felt a chill move across her skin. Her friend had always been lavish with her praise. But the last thing Ellie wanted was to be part of Bascom's plan.

&

"For someone who owns a resort, the woman sure doesn't seem to be the friendly sort," Sheldon observed.

Bascom started from where he leaned against a crate, taking a momentary breather from the backbreaking labor of unloading. Sheldon stood nearby and apparently had seen the wave and lack of response.

"She's had hard times of late. She lost her husband and now recently she's lost her grandfather. He's the one I did business with." He raised an arm from the crate and pushed his hair from his forehead. A visit to a barber would be high on his list of things to accomplish during the next few days. "I think she's probably friendly enough. We just arrived with an unexpected surprise. I'm not sure I'd feel any differently if someone invested my fortune all in one purchase. It would certainly be a shock."

"I see."

Bascom didn't like the tonality of Sheldon's response. It was almost as if he read into the statement something that wasn't there. He pushed off from the box and gingerly put weight on his bum ankle. "Let's finish up with this wagon. I'm ready to get off my feet and settle in for the night." His ankle had been healing nicely and hadn't been a problem, but this past week he'd set himself back. Especially today with all the unloading, he'd pushed his recuperation to the limit. If possible, he'd find a way for a long hot soak to soothe the throbbing appendage.

"Sounds good. From the aroma wafting out the door from the kitchen, I'm ready to call it quits and sit down to a nice meal."

A lot of the men had waved off the offer of food, anxious to return home or to move on. But a handful remained, and they were all famished after the long trip. Prissy ran outside and directed them to the pump where they could freshen up.

"Mama said to come in through the side door and to make yourselves comfortable in the dining room. Dinner will be served. . ." A frown twisted her features as she thought for a moment. "Promp-ly."

"Thank you, Priscilla." Bascom hid his smile at the young girl's earnestness. "But could you please tell your mother we'd best eat outside?"

Priscilla frowned. "Why?"

"We've worked hard all day. I'm not sure it would be a good idea for all of us to traipse into your mother's pretty dining room."

"Oh, 'cause you're dirty?" Understanding dawned on her young features. She was a perfect miniature of her mother—complete with a long tangle of black curls—until you got to her eyes. Where her mother's were a deep emerald green, Priscilla's were a soft light brown.

"Yes, that's exactly why."

"Mama won't care. We feed lots of dirty people here because of the salty lake and sand. Mama says that's just part of life on the Great Salt Lake." She leaned close. "A lot of them even stink 'cause of the algae. You smell lots better than some of our guests do."

Several of the men chuckled at her bluntness.

Bascom glanced at Sheldon, who shrugged.

"Well then, I think we'll take your advice and eat in the dining room. . .if you're sure."

"I'm sure," she called over her shoulder. Mission accomplished, she skipped back toward the main building.

Several of the men deferred on eating in the formal dining atmosphere and asked to be served their meal outdoors. Sheldon and Bascom joined the handful of guests that were left on the premises. Though the large room was elegant with ornate wall coverings and polished hardwood floors, the atmosphere was cozy and relaxed.

Ellie kept glancing at Sheldon, and a frown hovered in her eyes. When the last guest left the room, Bascom asked her about it.

"I've just realized your assistant will be staying with us, too. I haven't a room for him."

So that was it. "If it's all right with you, Sheldon will stay in the storage room off the building where we'll be working. It's just the right size for one person. He's already moved his things in there."

The tension drained from her shoulders. "That'll be fine. But what about the other men?"

"They'll all move on tonight. They're ready for a night in town. Only Sheldon and I will remain."

"Then that's settled. I feel much better." She still looked uncomfortable. "Thank you for understanding. Your arrival caught me by surprise."

"I noticed." He hoped his smile would soften the words. "But I do understand. You didn't exactly expect us, and with a full guest list, we put you in a rough spot."

Wanda began to clear the dishes while Ellie, Priscilla, and Mary led the way to the parlor. Sheldon made his excuses as they passed through the central hall, and loaded down with a lantern and other supplies he'd need for his new quarters, bid everyone a good evening. Bascom figured now was as good a time as any to finish up details with his hosts and settled down onto a soft rose-colored wing chair. It felt heavenly to take the weight off his ankle.

Ellie watched for a moment as he tried to find a comfortable place for his foot, then she hopped up to move a padded footstool in front of him. He lifted his foot and rested it carefully on top.

"Gram, Wanda, Priscilla, and I have our own private parlor at the back of the house. The area we're in now is the original house, but my grandfather added on the large extension at the side for guests when the area started booming as a tourist location a few years back. The guests are welcome to use this parlor and the front porch anytime they like, so please make yourself at home. Most guests are tired after a day of activity and retire to their quarters after the late meal."

Bascom nodded. "I aim to do the same myself soon. I'm ready for a good night's sleep."

Priscilla climbed onto Ellie's lap and snuggled into her arms. Her eyes were heavy. "Mama, is it Whimsy time? I'm tired."

Ellie lowered a kiss to the girl's soft curls before glancing his way. "It is. Let me finish up with Mr. Anthony first and make sure he has everything he needs."

"Please call me Bascom." Bascom disliked formal titles. Back east the lines of propriety were well defined, but he hoped those boundaries were dimmer this far out west.

"Bascom it is. Well. . .now that we have everything settled, do you require anything else before we retire for the night?" She hesitated and glanced down at his ankle. "Forgive me for intruding, but your ankle—it seems to be bothering you. You've worked hard today. Would you like to soak it?"

Wanda entered the room and overheard. "Of course he would! I'll set a pot of water to heat on the stove right now." She bustled back out, and they could hear pans clanging about in the kitchen.

Ellie turned to him with a smile. "That's taken care of then. When Wanda sets her mind to something, there's no talking her out of it."

"So I see. I didn't even have a chance to try." Bascom had the feeling she spoke from experience.

"Is there anything else we can do for you?"

"I'd love directions to a good barber. Will I find one in town?"

Mary's blue eyes brightened. "I'll do better than that. I'll cut it right here. Let me get my things."

"Oh no, I couldn't ask that of you. One more day won't hurt any." His voice tapered off as the elderly woman stood, and ignoring his words, hurried from the room.

Ellie smirked. "You'd best stop arguing right now. First thing you need to learn now that you're staying is that once Gram sets her mind to something, she doesn't back down easily—same as Wanda." She exchanged an amused glance with her daughter, and then looked back up at him, her eyes suddenly nostalgic. "Gram loves to cut hair. She misses fussing over Papa. It would be nice if you let her cater to you."

"Mama, my Whimsy tale?"

"All right." She mouthed a silent apology to Bascom for the interruption. "Once upon a time, in the Land of Whimsy,

Princess Priscilla woke up in a strange place. Nothing looked familiar. . .”

Mary returned and directed Bascom to a straight chair and went to work. Wanda set a large wash pan beneath his foot and filled it with steaming water. Bascom took advantage of the quiet and tuned in to Ellie's soft words as she spoke to her daughter of a private, magical world. As she painted word pictures of adventurous pirates, beguiling mermaids, and various sea creatures—some he'd heard of and some he figured were created from her imagination—he began to develop his plan for the carousel's theme into a fully detailed image.

three

Bascom woke at dawn and tested his weight on his ankle. He'd learned through experience that if he didn't exercise it, he'd be stiff later. The soak had done its job; the ache was mostly gone, and the appendage felt much better now after a rest. He gingerly dressed and stepped onto the front porch.

Mist hung over the lake in the early morning air, and he decided to walk closer to the water and explore. No one else was up and about at this hour. The quiet refreshed him, and he felt a peace that had been absent for a long time. The hustle and bustle of Coney Island seemed far away from this quaint place.

Even this early, Coney wouldn't have had a quiet or isolated place for Bascom to catch a thought. And there wasn't a moment that someone else hadn't been in sight, whether sleeping off too much imbibing from the night before or getting started early on the day's work.

He began to walk along the shoreline, his gait gaining steadiness as he went. He'd heard tell that the area was known as "the Coney Island of the West," but in his experience he didn't see any resemblance at all. The lake spread out before him, water as far as the eye could see. If he didn't know better, he'd assume by the vastness that it was open water like the ocean. But where the ocean roared toward the sand with mighty waves, the water here seemed gentler, lapping against the shore's edge.

A soft breeze drifted across the water. Mountains in the distance stood tall against the blue sky. The sun shone down, warming his shoulders and back. For the first time since losing his wife and son, he felt alive again. The warmth eased the iciness that had filled his heart for so long.

He thought about his newest carousel, the first since the accident, and wondered if his returning to work caused the burden to lift. But the burden had prevented him from working, his focus refusing to move past all the grief and all that had happened, until now.

Whatever the reason, Bascom rejoiced and savored the warmth that filled his soul. He whispered a prayer of thanks to God, with whom he'd recently started a relationship, for bringing him to this place of healing. Though his heart still ached over his losses, he knew he was on the path to recovery. The prompting he'd felt to take a new contract, this one specifically, was a good thing.

"Mr. Anthony. Mr. Anthony!"

Bascom stopped in his tracks as he heard the young voice calling from behind him. He turned to see a pink-enveloped Priscilla hopping along with a clumsy skip. The sight brought a smile to his lips.

She wasn't much older than his son had been, and both had the same enthusiasm about life. The pang of loss was with him, but Priscilla's arrival distracted him from dwelling on it.

She stood before him and grinned. Her plaited hair draped behind her back. Though her dress appeared to be new, her worn brown boots told a different story as she dug her wiggly heel into the soft sand at the water's edge. "I'm not s'posed to be down here without an adult. But you're an adult, right?"

He squatted to meet her gaze. "I am. Did you tell your mother or anyone else that you're out here? They might be worried if they can't find you."

"I told them I'd be out on the porch. . .then I saw you."

"So if they come outside, they're going to worry. They won't know you're with me."

She giggled. "Silly. They will if they look around like I did!"

"All the same, I'd feel better if we return and receive permission for you to be at the water's edge with me."

"Yes, sir." She sighed. "But they might make us stay to eat if we do that."

Bascom's stomach rumbled at the thought of a good, hot breakfast. "I can't think why that would be a bad thing. My stomach says it's a great idea."

Priscilla, apparently not having a shy bone in her body, reached up and clutched his hand. "Then let's go find your stomach some food." She stopped and looked up at him. "But can we walk to the water again later?"

"Only with your mother's permission."

"Yes, sir."

They rounded a slight bend, which brought the resort back into view. Ellie, arms crossed against her chest, strode toward them. She stopped as she saw her daughter clinging to Bascom's hand.

"Mama! How'd you know where to find us?" Prissy let go and skip-hopped to her mother's side where she threw her arms around the woman.

"I followed your footprints in the sand."

"I was with an adult."

"I see that. But you need to tell me next time."

"Mr. Anthony told me that. He was bringing me back."

Ellie addressed him for the first time. "I appreciate that. I'm sorry if she's been a bother. I hope she didn't intrude on your quiet time."

Bascom waved her words away. "She wasn't a bother at all. She's welcome to join me at any time"—he glanced down at the smiling little girl—"*if* she first receives approval from you."

Mother and daughter exchanged a look, and Ellie nodded.

"I suppose that will be fine."

"Thank you!" Priscilla buried her face in her mother's long skirt for a quick hug before returning to grasp Bascom's hand.

"Breakfast is almost ready. Can the walk be postponed until after?"

Bascom knew he needed to start work on the carousel after the morning meal, but when Priscilla's face fell with disappointment, he couldn't help himself from saying, "We can take a quick stroll after we eat. It's good for digestion. But I'll need to get to work soon after."

"Oh, she can wait until another time. Please don't let my daughter keep you from your work."

Bascom couldn't tell if her words were a reprimand, directing him to follow his contract and finish his work as soon as possible, or if she only spoke to give him a way out of walking the lakeshore with her daughter. Though he knew her rooms at the resort were at a premium and he took up one of them, he also knew the room he occupied wouldn't be rented out even if he left early, so he threw caution to the wind. Returning the smile to Priscilla's face took far more precedence than finishing the carousel a few moments earlier.

"We'll walk. I need to balance my time, and part of my work is getting to know you both so I can properly capture your essence in my project."

Ellie's eyes darted to his in mortification and then just as quickly looked at the lake.

He chuckled. "I didn't mean to embarrass you. But I do need to get to know you better if I'm to make the carousel work for your resort. You need to have a draw."

"I can't imagine what that draw will be. We're a simple sort."

Bascom had to disagree. There was nothing simple about the stunning woman that walked beside him. He wondered what had brought her to the point of believing such a thing.

She walked with an air of confidence, yet she seemed to shut herself off from the world around her. He felt sure she hadn't seen the beauty in the view before her for quite some time. Instead, her eyes focused on the building they moved toward while her thoughts remained far away.

"You just be yourself, and I'll create the draw."

Priscilla yanked his hand, bouncing up and down. "I love to draw. Can I draw the picture with you?"

Bascom chuckled. "Sure you can. The picture wouldn't be complete without you."

Ellie laughed softly. "There are different meanings to the word *draw*, Prissy. In this case, the word refers to a way to bring in more guests to the resort. We want to use the carousel to draw—or bring in—more business."

They watched as Priscilla sucked in her bottom lip with concentration. "Oh. And sometimes, Mama, you *draw* me bathwater from the pump."

"Exactly! So you can see there are different meanings to that word."

"Well, I'd rather you draw me a picture of a bath than make me take one." Her eyes took on a mischievous glint. "Or, Mr. Anthony could take me swimming in the lake, and I wouldn't have to bathe at all."

"I thought you said people came out of the lake all smelly from the algae," Bascom teased with a tweak to her braid.

Ellie's gasp caught his attention. "Prissy, you didn't!"

"Yes I did. They do stink sometimes, Mama."

Bascom wrinkled his nose. "And that's what you want to smell like after you bathe? I'm not so sure that's a very good idea."

"I guess not." She looked disappointed for a brief moment, then her eyes brightened. "I know! You can take me for a swim and then Mama can *draw* me a bath for after!"

Both adults laughed.

"Your daughter doesn't lack in negotiating skills. She'll be a fine businesswoman someday."

"I guess she will at that. Though I'm not sure her precociousness is a good thing at this age."

"Nonsense. You need to cultivate the trait in her from the start. How else will she learn to follow her heart—and do an about-face—if she's held back now?"

Ellie's sigh much resembled her daughter's. "I suppose you're right. But it is a hard balance to find."

"I think you're on the right track, and from what I've seen, you're raising a fine daughter here."

"Thank you."

Bascom turned his attention back to the little girl tugging on his hand. "And I'll have you know that in this case, though our attraction will create a *draw* for tourists, we also need to draw the ideas onto paper so I have a plan to work with. I'd still welcome your help with that."

"What kind of ideas?"

"Secret ones." Bascom put a finger to his lips and smiled. "Your mother can't see the final product until it's ready. If you assist me, you'll have to keep quiet on what we're creating."

Ellie looked worried. He understood. She didn't know him well. "And only the proprietor has to wait for the final unveiling. Miss Wanda and Mrs. Case are free to come and go as they please, as long as they promise not to tell any details."

Now she sent him a look of annoyance. "So this entire thing is about me, but I'm the one who can't see it until the unveiling?"

He nodded. Priscilla giggled.

"And what if I don't like the finished product?"

Bascom put a hand to his heart in feigned horror. "I've not yet found one client who isn't satisfied with the final result.

You'll dearly love the carousel I build. In fact, I dare say you'll be shoving the small children out of your way just so you can have the first choice of character to ride."

"Mama!" Priscilla's chagrined voice interrupted. "You wouldn't."

Ellie glanced down at her daughter. "You never know. According to your Mr. Anthony, I just might."

He liked this playful side of his employer.

Priscilla stared out over the water for a moment, contemplative, her brow furrowing with concentration before she whipped around to speak to them.

"Then I'll draw a special carving just for me to ride. I'll ask Mr. Anthony to make it too small for you to sit on."

Their laughter carried across the water, and Ellie pulled her daughter close for a hug.

"Is that what all that staring at the water was about?" Bascom teased. "I thought for a moment you'd become distracted from our conversation and were looking for a mermaid."

"No, silly."

"Oh, that's right, because mermaids are pretend?"

"No. It's because nothing like that can live in the Great Salt Lake. It's too salty and only tiny brine shrimp can swim in it."

"Ah. So I'd best put away my thoughts of breaking out my fishing pole and catching us all a good dinner."

Priscilla sent him a sideward grin. "You didn't *bring* a fishing pole, Mr. Anthony. I watched you unpack your wagons, remember?"

He ruffled her hair as they stepped onto the porch. "And how do you know I don't have one packed away in one of those many crates?"

Again her face creased in thought. "Oh."

She hopped up the several steps and thumped onto the hard planks that led to the front door. "Well, we can *draw* you one, and you could carve it."

"That's a fact." He grinned over her head at Ellie. "But what would be the point if now I know I'd never catch a fish?"

"Well, it would give you something to do while you sit and watch me swim." She smiled impishly and hurried through the front door. Ellie's laugh filtered back as she followed.

The general corruption and cutthroat competition between carousel designers back East on Coney Island seemed far away. For a short time the pleasant walk with Ellie and Priscilla had pushed the violence of his former life to the back of his mind. Whether the beautiful climate or the two females created a balm for his soul, he didn't know. But if time spent in their company would continue to make him feel alive again, he'd carve a fishing pole for each of them, just to give him an excuse to share their company. He'd always worked hard, and this job would be no exception, but he'd also have time to relax—and he intended to use his rest time to get to know his hosts better. Maybe in turn he could make Ellie's life a bit easier by helping out a bit.

He had a feeling he was going to like it here, and after two years of grief, healing might just come packaged in the duo that had entered the resort before him. He could only hope the tormentor who'd made his life a living nightmare had finally given up his quest for vengeance now that Bascom had moved out West.

four

Ellie shifted the pan full of green beans that rested on her lap and tried to focus on her daughter's words as she snapped the vegetables for dinner. She usually loved their early morning time together, but today she felt restless. Bascom had given Prissy a small wooden carousel horse to play with the evening before, and Prissy now sat at her feet on the worn planks of the porch, keeping up a continuous dialogue about the pony's adventures. With half her focus on listening to the little girl's rambling chatter, Ellie found herself watching for any sign of movement near the outbuilding and had to keep redirecting her thoughts away from the curiously interesting man.

She smiled as she acknowledged the fact that she was the curious one. She couldn't deny the fact that Bascom piqued her thoughts about where he'd come from, why such a kind man was alone in the world, and how he'd ended up with the limp. Had he been born with it? She didn't think so. His cautious steps made the injury appear to be a fresh one, still tender to movements or overwork.

Though he did work hard, even with the injured ankle, she quickly corrected herself. The man had definitely kept busy during the first week of his stay, so busy in fact that she'd hardly seen him, and according to both Prissy and Wanda, he'd made a lot of progress on his work. But at what expense to his health? Did he neglect and overwork his ankle in order to be out of her way since she'd made clear the hardship his arrival would cause the resort? In the end, they'd all shuffled over a bit, and he'd done nothing but liven up the place with his good humor during the few times she'd seen him. He did seem to be a very nice man.

"Mama, you're smiling. Do you like my story?" Prissy peered up at Ellie, her eyes squinted against the brilliant sunlight that filtered under the covered porch.

"I always love your stories. You know I do." Ellie answered, again having to refocus her thoughts away from the man and back onto her daughter.

Priscilla stared a moment longer. "You were smiling over at the big building. *Not* because of my story."

"Oh."

"I know what you were thinking about..." The amusement in Prissy's impish smile matched the amusement in her twinkling brown eyes.

"You do?" Ellie put a hand to her heart and patted it, flustered. If her young daughter could read her thoughts, how much more obvious must they be to any adult that might be watching?

"*You're* thinking about how to sneak in and take a peek at your new carousel." Prissy's giggle filled the air.

Thoroughly disconcerted over her wayward musings, Ellie sighed with relief. Maybe her silly notions weren't as transparent as she'd thought. "Oh, and is that what you'd be doing if things were flipped around and *you* were the one waiting for the surprise?"

"Yes, ma'am, it's exactly what I'd be doing."

Ruffling her daughter's hair, Ellie snapped the last bean and set the bowl aside. "Well actually, I was thinking about the new carousel *and* wondering how Mr. Anthony hurt his foot. It seems to be a new injury, and I'm wondering if he might need some doctoring or if he should even be up and about, walking on it as he does. *That's* where my mind had wandered off to. Though I was still listening to your story, and you can quiz me on that fact if you feel you must."

"No, I know you always listen." Prissy grew quiet as she followed her mother's stare at the building. "Do you think he hurts? He's nice. I don't want him to hurt 'cause of the carving."

"I'm not sure, but I think I'll ask him about it today at lunch."

"He injured it in a fire."

Both females jumped at the intrusion of Sheldon's voice as he walked around the corner of the house. His silent steps hadn't warned of his arrival, and Ellie couldn't help but wonder if he'd been eavesdropping.

He grinned. "Sorry if I startled you. I thought I'd take advantage of the early hour and do some exploring."

"Oh, I thought perhaps you were both already hard at work on the attraction." Ellie stopped, realizing her words sounded judgmental, as if the men should have been up and working away. "I mean, I hadn't seen either one of you, so I figured you'd made an early start." There she went again, her words insinuating they should have been doing just that.

Sheldon leaned lazily against the support post and waved her words away. His dusty boots attested to a stroll along the lake, but that didn't mean he hadn't been listening to what they'd discussed a few minutes before. She didn't like the thought.

"We have started early most days, but Bascom's ankle must be acting up because he wasn't out there this morning. I decided rather than mess something up by guessing what he'd want me to do, it would be better to wait and see what we'd be doing when he made an appearance."

"You mentioned a fire?" Ellie didn't mean to pry, but her concern for her guest overrode her better judgment.

"Yep." Sheldon, unasked, took the stairs two at a time and

pulled a chair close to Ellie's. She fought the urge to move hers a few inches in the other direction. His presence unnerved her. Partly due to the fact that they'd discussed Bascom behind his back, but also partly because he'd moved too close to her. She felt crowded in his presence.

Bascom always kept a polite and proper distance between them the few times they'd been together, during their walk and at meals. She preferred his standards to Sheldon's.

Though she felt smothered by his nearness, he obviously felt nothing of the kind because with his knee almost touching Ellie's he still leaned forward to close the space between them as he spoke.

"Coney Island has become very competitive between businesses, sort of like what you're experiencing here, but much worse. The area is thriving, and the resorts compete to keep the upper hand so that their place will be most popular the next year. The attractions are getting bigger and better, and the builders of the attractions are just as competitive as the people hiring them."

"Bascom doesn't seem the competitive sort." Ellie felt she needed to defend the man for some inane reason. Probably, again, due to the fact he wasn't around to defend himself as they gossiped.

"He's not. That was part of the problem. Crime has escalated right along with the influx of tourists."

"The vacationers are criminal?"

"No, not the vacationers. But the people that vie for their business aren't above finding ways other than attractions to force some of the business operators out."

Ellie gasped. "That's terrible."

"It is. Organized crime has moved in and now they work different operators and charge for their protection. At times, that 'protection' includes setting fires or using other methods to put an overly competitive neighbor out of business."

"And is that what happened to Bascom?" Ellie couldn't believe people would sink to such lows, but then again, she knew her desperation to keep her own resort afloat. That nature, she felt sure, drove some people to drastic and scandalous measures.

Sheldon reached over and tugged at her skirt in a most inappropriate manner. Her emotions must have reached her expression because he smiled and held up the end of an errant green bean for her to see. "Didn't want it to stain your pretty dress."

Ellie nodded, wanting him to continue and then be on his way.

"A little over two years ago, Bascom and I had just finished a carousel for a place on the beach, our most beautiful creation yet. Much like your competitor to the east. . ." He gestured in the direction of which he spoke.

"Saltair."

"Thank you. Much like Saltair, they had a dance pavilion, cottages for the guests, and a huge boardwalk that went out over the Atlantic Ocean. The carousel was the focal point, and people were scheduled to arrive the next week to see what Bascom had created. In the meantime, a corrupt man named John McKane controlled the area, and he often would ask for money in exchange for protection."

"And he did this to Bascom?" Ellie was horrified at the thought. She knew there were evil people in the world and that bad things happened to people who didn't deserve it. Her loss of her husband proved that. But she would never understand what drove people to purposely hurt others or how they could live with themselves if they did.

"Not directly. No one knows for sure who was behind the accident. But we have our suspicions." He glanced at Priscilla, who had moved to the far rail and now balanced her horse upon it while talking quietly to herself, and lowered his voice. "Bascom's family had arrived the day before, his wife and young son, and were free to enjoy the facilities during the week prior to opening. After a swim with the family, Bascom left them to enjoy the carousel while he went to nap. Like I said, we'd worked hard, and he took advantage of the break between projects to catch up. A fire started in the building that housed the carousel, a fast-moving and ferocious fire. Bascom's wife and son were trapped inside. By the time Bascom was summoned, it was too late. Bascom, out of control from grief, tried to get to them, but the few people that had arrived by that time held him back. He fought them, broke free, and entered the structure just as the roof collapsed, which trapped his ankle under the outer beam. The bystanders were able to pull him out."

"How awful!" Tears collected in Ellie's eyes and slipped down her cheeks. She didn't even try to hold them back. No one should ever have to endure such horror. Though she'd lost her husband, he'd been taken from her by natural causes. A severe illness had claimed his life. She lowered her voice to match his. "To watch your spouse and child burn to death in front of your eyes—I can't even comprehend."

Sheldon looked at her then looked off toward the out-building. "It's only fair to tell you—there was another version of the story that floated around for a time. I'm sure the authorities have dispelled their concerns on that one, though, or he'd be in custody by now, just like John McKane..."

"The city boss?"

"Right. He was arrested around this same time period for his criminal activities."

Ellie felt a shiver of apprehension pass through her. She didn't want to hear. Bascom, at this time, was her employee.

She felt the right to know if his injury would prevent him from successfully doing the job he'd been hired to do. But based on Sheldon's last words, they were now bordering on pure gossip, and she didn't like it. "Perhaps it's best we leave it alone if the authorities have cleared him."

"I feel you need to know. Hear me out for my peace of mind, and then do with the information as you please."

She nodded but felt like a traitor.

"The other story has it that Bascom himself set the fire and that he was injured during his escape."

"Are you insinuating Bascom had something to do with McKane? That he committed arson—and murdered his own wife and son—in order to prevent other businesses from succeeding?"

"I wasn't around at the time. We'd finished our job and didn't have another lined up yet. Though we had a lot of requests, Bascom hadn't chosen one."

"You're his friend and assistant. I've not known the man for long, but I have a hard time believing the man I've met would ever be capable of committing something as cold-blooded as the act you've just told me about."

"I have to agree. Like I said, I wasn't around at the time. I've only heard rumors, and I'm sure that's just what they are. But I felt I owed you both explanations for what happened. You deserve to feel safe here, and I'd hate to see bad things start happening to you."

The shiver returned, but Ellie couldn't tell what caused it. The fact that Bascom might have done exactly what the rumor insinuated? Or that his assistant's final words sounded almost like a threat?

She watched as he hopped up from the chair and dropped to his knee at Prissy's side. He glanced at Ellie with a covert smile. Then he asked Prissy what she'd named her magnificent creature, and the little girl giggled at his magnified antics when he requested a turn to play.

Bascom exited the kitchen door at that moment, carrying a plate piled high with breakfast foods. A look of concern crossed his features when he saw Sheldon at the far end of the porch. He quickly reined it in and sent Ellie a smile.

"May I?" He motioned to the chair beside her.

"Of course." Ellie watched as Bascom balanced the plate in one hand while moving the chair back to a proper distance away from her with the other. His light brown hair looked tousled, as if he'd forgotten to brush it upon awakening. More likely, according to its shine, he'd brushed it, and it preferred to flop about his head at will as usual.

She realized he stared back at her with an amused expression as he took his first few bites of food. His blue eyes twinkled over his private thoughts, and again she had a hard time believing that this man, who'd made her feel so at ease in his company, could ever hurt anyone.

He ate in silence for a few minutes, and she dug through her pan of beans to be sure she'd properly prepared them for cooking amidst all the distractions.

"Ellie." Bascom's soft voice caused her to glance up. A look of concern had replaced the amusement as he glanced from her to Sheldon and back again.

"Please be careful who you trust. Not all people are as they seem."

The shiver returned. She couldn't be sure whether his words referred to Sheldon—because his eyes again moved in that direction after the statement—or if he knew of their little chat and the words also referred to him.

Regardless, she'd take his words to heart and trust no one. That was the safest thing to do.

five

Please be careful who you trust. Not all people are as they seem.

Bascom's words echoed over and over in Ellie's mind. She considered their meaning as she did the laundry, her least-liked chore. She put a hand to the small of her back as she straightened from leaning over the washtub, forcing her aching muscles to cooperate. Though she'd risen early to begin her work, the washhouse heat caused beads of perspiration to roll down her face and back. Her dress wilted against her, and she couldn't wait to finish. Maybe she'd reward herself and Prissy with a swim later in the afternoon. The water would feel refreshing, even if they would have to rinse off afterward so the salt wouldn't cake on their skin.

She glanced out the small window where the morning sun had just begun to light up the sky. The day promised to be a beautiful one, with a brilliant blue sky and very few clouds. She felt alone in the world at this hour, with everyone else snuggling under their covers for the last hour or so of sleep. Though some guests trickled down early, most slept later than they usually would, savoring each moment of their visit.

A droplet of sweat ran down her forehead, and she used her sleeve to wipe it away. She shook away her musings and again bent over the washtub, anxious to get as much work finished as possible before Priscilla woke up and ran out to "help." Her thoughts again wandered to the two men staying on the premises. Surely her grandfather had investigated them thoroughly. He wasn't a man to make a rash decision, and she felt sure he'd have researched carefully before committing such a task—and such an amount of money!—to just anyone.

But none of it made sense, beginning with why her grandfather would even do such a thing with their inheritance. And even more alarming, why, if Bascom had meant she shouldn't trust Sheldon, would Bascom have the man working as his assistant? Surely she'd misconstrued his meaning. Sheldon seemed nice enough. Perhaps Bascom only meant that with so many strangers coming and going at the resort, she'd be well-advised to use caution as to who she spent time with since he'd seen her so easily visit with both Sheldon and himself. She also entrusted Priscilla to the men's company, but always under the supervision of Wanda or her grandmother.

She felt secure with such measures but would be sure to keep her daughter under one of the females' constant care. Times were changing, more guests were using their facility as word spread and as the community grew, and even though they had wonderful neighbors and townsfolk, bad people with ill intent usually interspersed with the good ones as towns expanded and strangers moved in. She'd do well to keep better track of her daughter, and in light of that, she welcomed Bascom's thoughtful words and advice.

Ellie decided she would read no more into his intent than that, a mere warning to be cautious with her trust. Growing up at the resort had built hospitality into her nature. Though it stretched her to warmly welcome strangers into her home, she'd become acclimated to doing just that, even if her personal level of comfort strained in the process. But in doing so, she'd also become overly trusting and tended to forget to keep in mind that not everyone who passed their way would be deserving of that trust. And even though Bascom had extended the warning, she'd do well to steer clear of him as much as possible as well.

After snagging up another armload of sheets, Ellie placed them in the water she'd carried from the pump. They'd rigged up an old stove years before to boil the water, and she'd already filled it with a measure of Ivory soap flakes. The handle on the washtub creaked in protest as she began to rotate it, the action forcing the paddles inside the barrel to mix the bedclothes around. As one arm began to ache, she switched to the other.

"If you'll step aside, I think I've found a way to make your chore a bit easier." Bascom spoke from the doorway directly behind her.

Ellie jumped as his voice intruded on her thoughts. Hadn't she just made the decision to steer clear of the man?

She straightened but was sure he didn't miss her stiffness upon reaching an upright posture. The wash water sloshed with the abrupt break in rhythm, then silence filled the room.

"Pardon?" Ellie, flustered by his appearance, pushed her hair away from her face. Quiet and private, the man had a way of staying in the background, doing his work, and letting others do theirs. His invasion into her work space felt personal.

Bascom motioned to a contraption he held in his hand. "There are easier ways to do some of the things that are done around a place like this. I watched you on laundry day last week and, though I know my time is to be spent on the carousel, it didn't take much effort at all for me to put this together." He hesitated. "I used my spare time in the evenings and my experience with the carousel to form a similar steam engine setup to help with your laundry chores."

"Really?" Intrigued in spite of herself, Ellie grinned at the thought. No one had ever done such a thing for her. "How does it work?"

"If you'll step aside, I'll rig it up and show you." He moved closer into the room, and Ellie rounded the washtub and backed toward the door. She stood in the doorway and relished both the break and the cool air that filtered past her.

She watched as he hooked the contraption to the handle of the washtub. "I'll use the same system you use to heat the boiling water to run this smaller version of the engine that will power your carousel." He continued to work as he spoke.

Priscilla arrived and greeted Ellie with a hug before slipping under her arm to peer inside at Bascom. "Whatcha doin', Mr. Anthony?"

Bascom paused and sat back on his heels, shifting a bit to accommodate his injured ankle. "I'm putting together a steam engine to ease your mama's load on wash day." He sent her a crooked grin that highlighted a deep dimple in his left cheek.

"Oh, can I help?"

"Sure. C'mon over here and hold this tube for me." He helped Priscilla grip the rubber tube before glancing over his shoulder toward Ellie. "Don't worry, we're not hooking up the steam yet."

Ellie appreciated the way he took time to acknowledge her daughter instead of continuing his work while offering his explanation—or worse, ignoring her questions completely. She also liked that he directed his reassurance to Ellie without making Priscilla feel unneeded.

Bascom spoke quietly throughout the process and patiently answered Prissy's many questions. With a warm chuckle he glanced at Ellie. "I think she'll be able to build her own as soon as we're finished here. It looks like I'm going to have competition in my business if I don't watch out."

Priscilla's delighted giggle filled the air. "I'm too little to do business."

"Is that so? You could have fooled me."

Prissy glanced at Ellie and rolled her eyes. Ellie responded in turn. They shared a conspiratorial smile.

"Great job!" Bascom stood and wiped his hands on his trousers. "Let's see how it works."

Ellie moved forward to watch. Bascom explained as he went. "The water will heat up, and the steam will put pressure on this piston and exert force. I've rigged it up like the process used to make the carousel horses move up and down. That same force will, in turn"—he grinned at Ellie and she felt her heart skip a beat—"turn the gears that make the washtub do the job all on its own."

As he spoke, the process did just that, and Priscilla jumped up and down with excitement. Ellie just barely restrained herself from doing the same.

"Pure brilliance, that's what it is!" Ellie stepped closer, enthralled. "But how decadent to allow a machine to do my work for me."

This time Bascom let loose a laugh that startled them all. "I hardly think you'll be a lady of leisure with just this indulgence. You'll still need to gather the laundry, create the steam, load the linens into the tub, and hang them to dry. The upside is you'll be able to do most of that while the washtub does the most strenuous task for you. You'll be less tired. Now c'mon, give it a try."

She didn't even try to contain her smile as she moved forward and sailed through the process. He moved to do the same setup with the wringer, and before she knew it she had a full load ready to be aired in the slight breeze. The most remarkable part was that she could do just that while the next load churned away without her.

ዳ

"Thanks for letting me invite Mr. Anthony along on our swim trip, Mama!" Prissy skipped ahead, and her voice carried back to where Ellie and her carousel builder friend followed at a more sedate pace.

Ellie glanced at Bascom. He raised an eyebrow in amusement, and she quickly looked away. "It's the least we could do after he freed up my time so we could enjoy the afternoon."

"That's the only reason you asked?" His tonality revealed he was just as startled as she by his choice of words.

She kept her eyes forward, telling herself it wouldn't do to trip on a stone and sprawl flat on her face. But she knew her real reason for not meeting his eyes was the emotional reaction she felt every time their gazes met. While her intentions to keep him at a distance were sincere, her heart and daughter and every circumstance about them seemed determined to throw them into each other's path at every turn.

"What other reason would I have?" Her question, asked innocently, caused him to scowl.

"I'd like to think you might enjoy my company, too."

"Well, there's that, I suppose." She glanced at him just long enough to quirk her mouth into a teasing grin. She couldn't deny that he intrigued her or that she'd enjoy his company while Prissy splashed about in the water. "But I do want to thank you for lightening my load. I never dreamed such a thing possible. Your steam-powered washtub is simply amazing."

"I can't take the credit for inventing the steam engine, you know." He waved as Prissy hopped along backward, gesturing for their attention. "I can only take credit for having the right parts to make it work for this situation."

"Well, even so, it's wonderful, and I do appreciate it."

"Just make sure to keep it oiled as I showed you. Don't add too much at a time or it might splatter over the wash."

"I'll remember. Just a few drops to keep it lubricated."

Prissy dropped to the ground and began to pull off her boots. Ellie hurried to join her, knowing patience wasn't her daughter's strongest virtue and if they dallied she might jump in boots and all. Bascom joined them, pulled a blanket from the basket he'd brought along, and expertly flapped it into the air so it settled flat on the small beach that abutted the shore.

Ellie kept one eye on her daughter while helping Bascom unload their picnic lunch. Surprised, she marveled over how at ease she felt in the man's presence. While in business mode, she managed to appear halfway intelligent, but in social situations, her tongue became mired in knots and she usually tripped over her words.

"You're not joining us?" Bascom nodded toward Prissy where she bobbed and dipped in the lake.

"Not today. I originally intended to, but. . ."

"My presence interfered?" A shadow of concern passed through his eyes.

"No, actually, the salt irritates my skin, and I'd have to bathe again. . ." She stopped midsentence, mortified that she'd blathered about such a personal situation, so comfortable was she in his presence.

"To remove the salt, I understand." Bascom finished her sentence casually without making her feel any more ill at ease.

"Exactly." She busied her hands setting out more of their lunch. "And since you made my morning so much easier, I don't feel the need to cool off as much as relax and enjoy my newfound leisure."

"Then I'll let you get to it while I go swim with that bobbing cork of a girl. Don't you worry about her being out there alone?"

He looked confused.

"It's the salt. You'll see once you immerse yourself. The buoyant quality of the water won't let you submerge, even if you try. You'll pop right back up to the surface. The lake is also known for its medicinal benefits. It will benefit your ankle, and you'll feel better for it."

"Sounds nice. And fun. I believe I'll try it right now. You just relax." He nodded toward her book and headed out to join Prissy where the little girl's gleeful shout welcomed him.

જ

Later, Bascom reclined and watched mother and daughter interact from between his partially open eyelids. He enjoyed their camaraderie and playful personalities. He knew from his own experience that life as a widower wasn't easy, but having Prissy certainly seemed to soften the edges of grief for Ellie. He knew the child's presence also brought additional challenges, and he was glad he could lighten Ellie's load in this small way and allow her more time to spend with her little girl. For the first time in more than a year, he allowed himself to fall into a deep sleep.

He awakened to Ellie's soft hand on his shoulder. "The sun's moved. We need to head back."

Priscilla slept beside him, curled up against his side. He didn't want to move. The scent of her sweaty, salty little-girl skin washed over him, and Ellie's eyes softened as a small smile curved her lips. He liked being in their presence and wanted the moment to last forever.

"She looks so content. I hate to wake her," Ellie said as she moved to do just that.

Bascom stopped her with a hand to her arm. "Then don't. I'll carry her if you'll gather up the blanket."

"I can't let you do that with your sore ankle."

"You can and will. She can't possibly weigh much more than that basket did when full. My ankle is much better, and it feels good as new after my soak."

"I think that's a stretch, but if you're sure. . ." Ellie studied him a moment. "You'll let me know immediately if it begins to bother you?"

Bascom nodded. He knew he wouldn't admit any such thing. Though his ankle did feel good enough, he doubted it would be an issue. Prissy snuggled against his chest, and his heart hitched. A throbbing ankle would be well worth this special moment in time. He'd lost his chance to enjoy such pleasures with his own son and wife. Back then, time had seemed to stand still and he had everything to look forward to in his future. He worked hard and spent too much time away from his loved ones, knowing they always had tomorrow. But he'd been wrong. Their tomorrows had run out, and all he had left were empty dreams he would never live to see. God had removed him from his grief, and for now this moment felt near enough to what he'd dreamed about before he lost the two most precious people in his life. If he'd learned anything, it was to savor the special moments as they came.

six

Bascom carefully worked to carve out the shape of a mermaid. He blew to clear off the dust and wood chips that had settled in the various nooks and crannies. A miniature replica of the carousel piece rested upon a table at his side, the finished painted object a map for this creation. He'd already decided that upon finishing the merry-go-round, he'd put the sample pieces into a miniature carousel for Priscilla to play with. She could remove them for individual play or attach them together and, with the help of a small motor he'd fabricated, watch as the tiny figures mimicked the movements of the amusement that would reside in the building outside her window.

Pleased with the thought, he stood and tucked the tiny mermaid out of sight. Prissy arrived at the most inopportune moments, and he had to work hard to keep her from seeing the miniscule replicas. He'd already given her a few of the standard horses, a move that had kept her attention from the other models that lay around at times. So far she'd proven herself to be trustworthy with their plans, an accomplishment most five-year-olds would find impossible to achieve.

The outer door opened, and Bascom glanced over to see Sheldon walk in from a break.

"Hey, boss, what do you want me to work on next?"

Sheldon's question grated against Bascom's nerves. He'd asked his assistant numerous times to refrain from addressing him in such a manner. They'd worked together for years, and the title had become unnecessary in Bascom's opinion. But they were now to a point where Bascom ignored the annoying word.

"You've finished the seahorses?"

"Yes. The paint should be dry, and if so they're ready to put into place."

Bascom rose from his stool and stiffly walked to where the two pieces rested. They were magnificent. "These are your best work yet, Sheldon, and you've done a lot of good pieces."

The praise came easily. Sheldon had proven himself to be a worthy carver, and Bascom felt sure it wouldn't be long until the apprentice moved on and began to carve a name out on his own. He grinned at his unintentional pun.

"Thank you."

Bascom looked around. "We're down to only a few pieces. I'll let you take your pick." He moved to the table with their sketches.

Sheldon perused them and plucked up a drawing of a simple horse. "I think I'll take this one for now."

"Then I'll let you get to it."

He watched as Sheldon stepped over to walk amongst the finished pieces they'd transported from their warehouse back East. Most of the basic horses were carved and ready to paint, but they'd waited to paint them until deciding on the theme. After matching the number on the drawing with the proper horse, he moved the piece over to the painting area.

Bascom returned his focus to his own piece. Since this part came naturally to him, without needing much thought, he talked to God as he carved. It wasn't long ago that he'd cut God out of his life. But after the darkness of losing his wife and son had subsided some, a pastor friend had spent several weeks pulling Bascom from his grief and bringing him teachings which restored his hope and drive to move on.

Though it hadn't been easy, the memories and pain dimmed, and good memories and peace filled the void his losses left behind. The pastor taught him a lot, and Bascom read the Bible continuously during those final weeks of their time together. By the time his friend needed to move on, Bascom had given his life to the Lord and vowed to live for Him, a promise he'd kept and intended to keep forever.

He knew the hard times were far from over. Memories would sneak up out of nowhere and send Bascom spiraling into a grief that set him back for days. When that happened, Bascom spent more time in the Word so that he would continue to grow and not lose sight of the God that loved him. It had worked up until now, and with this new stage, stepping out of the haven of familiarity where he'd grown up and married and loved and lost, he knew more adventures were in store.

The sky darkened outside their window, and Bascom realized he'd worked nonstop for several hours. He set aside his tools, dusted the mermaid, and nodded with satisfaction at the workmanship. She was developing just as he'd hoped. He froze as he realized the character's face mimicked Ellie's own. Mortified, he wondered what she'd think about being immortalized into the shape of a mermaid for everyone to see and for guests from all around to ride. She was such a quiet woman; she most likely wouldn't take too kindly to his recreating her into an amusement piece. Oh well. He couldn't change it now. Perhaps he could paint the features different than hers, but his will resisted that thought. He wanted his masterpiece to resemble the object of his inspiration. He'd find a way to highlight the mermaid without insulting or offending his employer.

Sheldon had already left the building while Bascom contemplated his deep thoughts. Dinner would be ready soon, and Bascom had taken to visiting with Ellie on the front porch during the short period prior to the evening meal. He had just enough time to freshen up in his room before meeting her.

๛

Ellie leaned closer to her work and caught up a small bit of fabric with the needle before pulling the thread away, closing the gap in the small tear. The pile of mending in the basket beside her had dwindled during the afternoon, and she realized how much Bascom and Sheldon's help at the resort freed her up to get other things accomplished. She and Wanda had stared at this basket for months, and neither one had the time to make a dent in the pile of linens that rested inside. But now she had only one more and would actually reach the bottom of the pile! Wanda, in the meantime, had more time to do what she loved best—to dabble in the kitchen formulating new creations to bring the guests back to their table over and over.

Sheldon supplied the woodshed with cut logs while Bascom found other heavy work to assist with. The barn sparkled. The horses' coats glistened. Delivery wagons from town were unloaded within minutes of their arrival and the goods placed strategically where they were needed. Neither man would accept Ellie's or Wanda's directions to stop and focus on the carousel. According to both men, they could only do so much in a day before needing to do manual labor in order to free their creativity so they could be productive again the next day.

Ellie had her doubts about whether the words were the complete truth, but regardless she appreciated their hard work and assistance. She also secretly enjoyed her evening discussions with Bascom on topics ranging from current politics to what folks were wearing and doing back East. Bascom seemed open to discussing anything she wanted to talk about, and with the constant influx of guests from all over, there wasn't ever a shortage to her list.

She knotted the thread and snipped it loose from the finished piece. Just yesterday they'd talked about his training in carousel carving and design, and only after she'd broached the subject of his wife and son had he shut down. She promised herself she'd be more careful of topics in the future, as she still felt the pain of losing her husband and grandfather, and she didn't want to cause Bascom similar grief.

"Mama, look at my spinning!"

Ellie glanced at her daughter, allowing her eyes to adjust from her detail work, and enjoyed the little girl's glee as she spun in circles on her swing. The contraption was another of Bascom's ideas. He'd hung two pieces of rope high in the branches of a tree and had formed a plank into a seat for Prissy to sit upon. She loved for someone to push her whenever possible, but otherwise contented herself with lying on her belly and flying into the air with a push of her feet or sitting upon the seat and twisting the rope before leaning backward as the swing spun around in circles.

"That's wonderful spinning, Prissy. I'm afraid one of these days you're going to spin yourself free of that tree and spin off into the sky."

Her daughter's giggle bubbled over to her. "That's not poss'ble, Mama."

"Whew, I'm glad to know that. You had me worried." Ellie sent her a teasing smile and reached for the final piece of mending. At this rate, she'd have the burdensome chore finished before Bascom's arrival. What a nice feeling that would be! She looked forward to evenings of watching Priscilla play or visiting with her guests without feeling like the mending loomed over her.

She heard footfalls on the path and smiled with anticipation. Bascom usually approached through the house, but today he must have changed his plans.

"Good evening," a deep voice called out. The voice didn't belong to Bascom. She glanced up in confusion and paused with her needle midair.

"Oh, good evening to you." She quickly stood and smoothed her skirt. Priscilla had stopped swinging and now sat watching the newcomer with curiosity. "I'm sorry. We weren't expecting any new arrivals. But we do have a room available if you're in need of one."

The man waved her words away. "No need to bother yourself. I've just come to introduce myself. I've hired on over at your neighbor's establishment and wanted to offer my services to you, too."

A tingle of suspicion ran along Ellie's back. She didn't know why, but the man unnerved her. Perhaps it was his sudden arrival, much like Sheldon's at times—so silent that she didn't know he'd come until he spoke. It was almost as if he'd wanted to look things over before making his presence known.

"Your services? I'm afraid I don't understand."

"Allow me to explain." Without an invite, he climbed the steps of the porch and settled into the chair next to hers.

Ellie fought the urge to wave him away and turn down his offer before he even voiced it. She already knew she didn't want the burly man working anywhere around her resort, her daughter, or the other ladies that lived with them. She settled back into her chair but hoped Bascom would make his appearance sooner rather than later.

❧

Bascom took the back stairs two at a time and entered the back hall in a rush. Mrs. Case had just exited the doorway that led to the ladies' private quarters, and she squealed as he nearly ran her down.

He caught her by her arms and gently steadied her. "I'm so sorry."

She stared over her glasses at him with knowing eyes and smiled. "Well, somebody certainly seems to be in a hurry."

"Yes'm. I am. I'm usually out front talking with Ellie by now, and I don't want to keep her waiting."

"Ah, it's a good man that abides by a customary routine. I'm sure she'll be delighted at your diligence and is waiting in anticipation, but you might slow down or you'll scare her with your intensity."

"Yes'm." He echoed his previous statement, wishing the woman would move on and allow him to be on his way. He adored Ellie's elderly grandmother, but now wasn't the time to chat. With her anyway. He knew if he didn't hurry, Sheldon would take his place on the porch, if he hadn't already.

"Go on now. And try not to run anyone else down in your hurry to get out front."

He could have sworn he heard her snort with a laugh as she walked away. Bascom felt an unusual flush flow up his neck. His actions were too transparent. But he couldn't deny the pull Ellie had on his heart, nor his attraction to his pretty host. If everyone else saw it, so be it. As long as Sheldon didn't feel the same way about her. And to prevent that, he needed to beat him to the chair. *The* chair. The one that should belong exclusively to him because it rested nearest hers.

He entered his quarters through the kitchen and splashed water over his face before toweling it dry. He grabbed a comb, pulled it through his hair, and splashed his hair with a dash of water when it wouldn't cooperate and lie right. The uncooperative strands cost him another few precious moments. He felt compelled to hurry and wondered if God prodded him in an effort to save Ellie from Sheldon's company. After changing into a clean shirt, he left the room at a safer pace, but still moved forward as he buttoned the white fabric into place. He stepped into the parlor and muttered under his breath as he heard a male voice droning away from the direction of the porch.

Maybe it was just a guest passing time with Ellie until supper. Who could blame him? With her sweet charm and feminine ways, she had a habit of making every guest feel special. But maybe the voice belonged to Sheldon. If so, Bascom would have to resort to alternative means to keep the ~~man working late~~ from now on so that he, Bascom, would be able to claim the coveted chair on the porch first. The jealous thought startled him. He didn't know where it came from, but decided to leave it for further exploration at a later time.

The closer he moved to the door, though, the more his hair stood up on the back of his neck. The voice didn't belong to Sheldon, and from his body's natural reaction, he didn't think it belonged to a pleasant guest, either. Bascom stopped just short of the door, listening to the man on the other side.

"So, if you'll pay me a small fee, I'll make sure no harm comes to you, your guests, or your fine establishment."

Ellie's soft gasp filled the air. "You're telling me someone is purposely damaging the area's resorts? What would be the purpose?"

"Ma'am, just because people like you and I are decent folk doesn't mean there aren't bad folk lurking about, too."

Bascom could hear Priscilla singing slightly off tune near her swing. He prayed she couldn't hear the man's words. Unbidden, images from his life on Coney Island came barging back into his memory; memories of a man in a similar fashion trying to get them to pay for his protection, memories of the madman competitor who made their lives miserable, memories of his wife and son dying in the fire. A fire that had been set as a trap for Bascom, and a fire that his loved ones had walked into instead. The killer had never been caught or punished—a fact that was a constant thorn in Bascom's side and one he tried over and over to set at the foot of the cross.

More often than not, though, he'd hurry back over and

pick up the burden once more, figuring it was his to carry for his lack of foresight or action. He determined the same fate would not come to Ellie, Priscilla, Wanda, or Mary. He returned to his room, pulled a small gun from his satchel, and secured it into the back waistband of his trousers, his dinner jacket hiding it from sight.

Upon returning to the door, he heard the man speak again. "You really need to reconsider. My price is fair for the service I provide. You don't want to live in fear on your own premises."

Bascom slammed the door open, and he felt a jolt of satisfaction when the man startled before turning in his seat to face him.

"The lady said she doesn't want your services." Bascom stated the comment in a firm voice, accentuating the last word for emphasis. "She's hired her own help and doesn't have need for outsiders."

Ellie raised her eyebrows at him in confused amusement, but the action didn't hide the concern and fear that had been on her face upon his arrival.

The man stood to his feet and moved closer to Bascom. "Oh really. And you're the one that's going to protect her?" His scorn, evident in the way he talked and looked Bascom over, turned Bascom's stomach. A man like him shouldn't be within a mile of Ellie or her resort. Bascom didn't have time to analyze his own defensive attitude. Ellie and her family had become his friends and no matter what, she deserved his loyalty and protection.

"Yes, I am. And based on that, I'll have to ask you to leave the premises."

The man stepped closer still. "Who's gonna make me?"

Bascom reached behind him, pulled his gun free, and shoved it against the burly man's chest. "I am."

Ellie stood and backed away from the two men.

The man paled and stepped backward, his hands raised in surrender. "No need to go over the edge, mister. I'll take my leave. But mark my words. By refusing my offer of protection, you've opened yourself up to all kinds of danger."

Bascom kept the gun leveled at the man's chest. "That sounds like a threat."

"Take it as you want." The sinister man stomped down the stairs and stalked away up the path toward their nearest neighbor's place. "Bad things are happening to folks up and down the shores of the lake."

Most definitely, Bascom would treat it as a threat. First thing the following morning he'd be in town, discussing it with the sheriff.

"Where on earth did you get that awful weapon?"

Ellie's distraught question broke into his thoughts.

"I always carry a weapon when I travel. It wouldn't be safe to travel any other way."

"Well, of course, but even with your full caravan of men? Surely their presence alone would ward off any thieves?"

Bascom sighed. "I wish you were right, but you aren't. That man there should be proof that you can't trust anyone, anywhere."

"But what if Prissy would have found it? She could have been hurt. We have guests to consider, also." Though she lowered her voice to a whisper, her pitch rose with anger.

"Ellie, calm down." Bascom took her by the arm and led her to her chair. She shook, whether from anger at him or from fear concerning the man who had just left, he didn't know. "I keep it in my satchel on a high shelf that Prissy can't reach. I always keep my door locked when I'm not in there. Priscilla is safe. Remember, I'm a father. . . . I was a father. I know about safety and children."

"All the same, I'd feel better if you kept it off the premises.

Could you at least keep it out at the pavilion?"

Amusement curled his lip. "Pavilion?"

Though she fought a smile, it peeked through. "Yes, pavilion. We can't very well keep calling the carousel's roost 'that outbuilding,' now can we?"

"I suppose we can't." Bascom opened the gun's chamber and spilled the bullets into his hand. "And I'll keep this out there if you prefer, but I strongly caution you to reconsider. If that man is any indication, we're in for some rough times ahead. It would be best if the gun resided within easy reach if that's the case. Men like that strike in the dark of night, not during the day when I'd have easy access to the weapon in the *pavilion*."

Ellie rolled her eyes at his use of the word. "Very well. Keep the gun in the house, but please use every precaution to keep it away from Prissy."

Bascom nodded and glanced at the little girl. Having missed the altercation, she innocently dug in the dirt with a stick while hanging from the swing by her stomach. Her sweet song reached his ears. As he watched, she glanced up at him and grinned. He waved, and she waved back. He'd do anything in his power to keep the little girl—and her loved ones—safe.

seven

Another week passed ~~with~~ no return visit from the offensive neighbor. Each day without vandalism or a threat brought Ellie a measure of peace. Though she'd not had problems in the past, the strange man's threatening behavior and words concerned her. The previous night Bascom had again waved off her fears. He assured her he and Sheldon would be on the lookout for anything out of the ordinary and that the women shouldn't concern themselves with things that couldn't be changed.

"Bascom, I've thought about it a lot since our last discussion and I still can't come to terms with why the man would be so forceful about his protection." No matter how hard Ellie tried, she couldn't let the topic drop.

With a sigh, Bascom scooted his chair back from the dinner table. "I didn't want to bring this up, but I guess it can't be avoided. When we worked on Coney Island, there were a lot of 'wars' between competing resorts and restaurants. The town became corrupt, and men of ill repute took over. They had a lot of pull with the governing men and began to bribe owners of various establishments with requests of payment in return for their protection." He hesitated and looked at Ellie, as if waiting for her to encourage or discourage him from going on with his explanation.

Ellie nodded and motioned for him to continue.

"Unfortunately, the men demanding the fees for protection were actually the ones the owners needed to fear most. Most likely, that man is one of them. He's capitalizing on the way things were back East. If an owner refused to pay, the men would damage the business in one way or another."

"Such as?" Ellie knew her face reflected her feelings of disgust at the thought. Instead of neighbors helping neighbors, as she was accustomed to here on the lake, those very bonds would be stretched to the limit in such a scenario. She found it very sad to think about.

"Such as fires were set. Buildings burned down. Rumors were spread about good, decent people to drive away their legitimate guests. Anything and everything that could be used to ruin the reputation would be put into play."

"That's horrible. Despicable! Why?" Ellie felt sick to her stomach.

"Nothing more than greed. When a person desires what he cannot have and he doesn't have a solid foundation of training to carry him through the tough times, he'll do terrible things that previously wouldn't have been considered."

"And this solid foundation. . .what does that entail? Admittance to the right schools? An education? A proper upbringing in the right family? What sets a person on that course?"

"A lack of faith, improper upbringing with no moral training—there are lots of reasons a person will turn to that lifestyle, but riches and education aren't at the top of the list. I'm sure they'd contribute. If a person is poor enough or resentful of others that might have better educational training, I'm sure he can find a reason to justify his poor behavior. But by solid foundation, I'm referring to spiritual training, faith in Jesus, and good morals."

"I see." Ellie contemplated the way she brought up Priscilla. The little girl acted like an angel, very rarely throwing a fit over anything, but did she miss out by not having the spiritual training Bascom referred to? Would her daughter's lack of spiritual training cause her to become like the vandals he referred to back East? Ellie's grandparents had always read the Bible as part of their daily routine, but Ellie's parents hadn't done the same. Though Ellie was familiar with her grandparents' faith, and she felt their beliefs were a nice guideline as a model of how to live one's life, Ellie hadn't been brought up that way before coming to live with her extended family as a young adult. At first she'd made an effort to understand and do as they did, but the daily practice of their routine had never completely taken with her; in time she'd let herself drift away. "Do you think I'm doing Priscilla a disservice by not reading the Bible to her on a regular basis?"

Bascom's expression gentled, and he laid his hand upon hers. "I think it's always a good habit to start for everyone, no matter what the reader's age."

He meant her, she could tell. She wondered if he thought her a bad person. Here she'd spent hours and hours weaving stories of whimsy to her daughter, but she'd sorely neglected her daughter's spiritual training.

"The habit of reading is important, but building a relationship with Jesus, as the Bible instructs, is what matters most."

Before Ellie could voice another thought, shouts sounded from outside. Bascom flew to his feet and headed out the door, and Ellie followed close at his heels. Mary and Prissy stood near the door to the private family quarters, while Wanda hurried into the hall from the kitchen.

"What's all the commotion I hear?" Wanda asked, her hands still coated in flour from supper preparations.

"I'm not sure," Ellie replied, motioning to the door that had slammed shut behind Bascom. "We heard shouting."

They moved forward to the door and peered out. Nothing seemed amiss. Ellie motioned for her grandmother to stay behind with Priscilla, and she and Wanda stepped onto the porch. From there they could see billowing puffs of smoke rising from the far corner of the pavilion.

"The pavilion's on fire!" Ellie yelled, catching up her long gray skirt in her hands as she ran for the pump. She grabbed a bucket and began to fill it while Wanda scurried around, gathering up more.

The air crackled and Ellie could hear the fire popping as it ate at the dry wood of the older building. She thought of all Bascom's hard work sitting inside, the wood pieces representing her grandfather's fortune, and pumped for all she was worth.

Scorched, wood-scented air filled Ellie's nose, and she sent up a hollow prayer for help. The words felt empty and seemed to fall on empty ears, too. She had no idea if God heard the prayers of those who hadn't talked to Him for such a long time. But surely one had to start somewhere and He understood that.

They pumped hard and filled each bucket as Bascom and Sheldon ran back and forth to douse the flames. The fire had been caught early enough that they were able to put it out before it caused substantial damage.

Bascom rounded the corner a final time, his face smeared with soot and sweat, and motioned for them to stop filling buckets. "I think we caught it in time. I'll watch it this afternoon and tonight to make sure it doesn't restart, but I think we got it all out."

Gram and Priscilla joined them as they surveyed the aftermath.

Prissy seemed fascinated with the whole process, which concerned Ellie and made her more determined to see to the child's spiritual training. They'd continue their Land of Whimsy tales, but they'd study the Bible each evening first.

Ellie didn't have a clue where or how to start, but she knew her grandmother would be happy to guide them.

≈

Ellie watched from her chair on the back porch as Bascom scrubbed the soot from his face by the pump. His clothes were ruined, but she'd insisted he change so Wanda could try to salvage them by soaking the scorched odor from the fabric. He walked over to her, and she noticed his face glowed a bright red. She hurried to her feet. "You're burned."

"No. I'm only flushed from the heat. I'll be fine as soon as I rest a bit." He settled into the chair beside hers. "I need to keep an eye on the pavilion, but I'll be able to see any smoke that starts up from here."

"I'll be right back." Ellie slipped into the kitchen and poured lemonade into a mug. The beverage was cool since Wanda had just made it up fresh from the pump's cool water. She stepped back outside and handed it to him. "Drink this. I'll only be a minute."

Ellie slipped inside again, this time to get the soothing liniment they used for burns. She returned, and Bascom eyed the ointment warily. "You're not slathering that on my face."

"Oh yes I am, and you're going to let me." If there was one thing Ellie could handle, it was a cantankerous man who didn't want to admit he needed nursing. Between her grandfather and her husband, she'd dealt with her share of stubborn males.

Bascom glared but didn't say anything more. She dipped her finger into the tin and rubbed her hands together to equally disburse the cream. "Look up at me."

"I'm gonna stink so bad no one will want me at the table tonight." Though he growled the words, he did as he was told.

"Quit complaining. There isn't a scent to this at all. If anything, your face will shine a bit, but after everyone hears about what a hero you are, no one will give your face another thought."

"No one needs to know about the fire or about my putting it out with Sheldon, ya hear?" Bascom, agitated, jumped to his feet. "I don't want to hear another word about it."

Ellie stood and watched in shock as he jumped from the porch, stalked to the pavilion, and disappeared around the far corner.

"Well, he certainly has a bee in his bonnet."

Sheldon's voice startled Ellie again. How was it he always seemed to creep up on her when she least expected it? Perhaps because she always so heavily focused on Bascom when he was around—or a lot of times even when he wasn't—that her thoughts weren't directed toward what went on in proximity to her. She told herself to concentrate more on the activity around her, especially now that they'd been vandalized. Or had they? Maybe the fire had started out of pure coincidence or chance.

"Sheldon, what—or who—do you think started that fire?"

"Coulda been most anything, I suppose." He climbed the steps and leaned against the rail, keeping his distance this time.

"Do you think it's possible it started on its own? Just a random spark or something? Did either of you leave a lantern burning out there when you left for lunch?"

Sheldon looked at her with amused eyes. "In broad daylight? We don't often leave a lantern burning throughout the day. There's plenty of natural lighting in the pavilion for us to work without wasting fuel and effort."

"Oh. You have a good point." Ellie frowned and stared at the building.

She didn't have the answers, and neither did the men. Staring wouldn't bring anything further to mind. She turned her attention back to Sheldon, who was remarkably untouched by the event. His clothes were none the worse for wear, and he didn't look the least bit flushed or burned. But in his defense, he'd mostly been the one to run back and forth for buckets, so he hadn't been as close to the heat or scorch of the fire.

She hated to ask her next question, but it needed to be voiced. "Do you think the act could have been the vandals the man from last week mentioned?"

Sheldon nibbled on a piece of grass he'd snagged somewhere on his walk. "I suppose anything is possible. Except. . ."

"What?" She stared hard at him. "Don't hold back any information from me. If you know something, I need to be told."

He glanced at the pavilion, consternation on his face. "I know, but this is hard."

She watched as he contemplated her request without answering. She reiterated her request. "I really need to know everything that's going on or that might be going on. Even if you don't think it's significant, I need to know."

Several emotions passed across his face as he carefully chose his words. "It's not that it isn't significant, but I owe a loyalty to Bascom. He's trained me well, and he's been good to me. I don't like to gossip about him."

"Bascom? What does he have to do with this? He worked hard to save the building and everything in it." Ellie's confusion pulled her mouth into a frown. She corrected it, not wanting Sheldon to know where her emotions lay.

"He might have nothing to do with the fire, and he might have everything to do with it."

Ellie's patience wore thin. "Out with it, Sheldon. What are you trying to say? Indirectly, you work for me, too. You owe me a certain loyalty as long as you're here. I have a small daughter. If you have any concern about a safety issue, I need to know it now."

Sheldon raised his eyes and peered into hers with a coolness that caused a shiver to run up her back. Though his hat sat low on his forehead, his eyes looked like black orbs in the added shade of the porch. "I'm concerned because a similar fire broke out at the pavilion back East, just before the bigger fire that killed Bascom's wife and child."

"So someone could be harassing him. Maybe someone set him up and is doing it again?"

"Maybe." Sheldon tossed the weed to the ground. "But why? The authorities scrutinized him while we were back East. They found no enemies, other than those jealous of his success. There were quite a few of them, but they were all cleared. Though competitive, they were all upstanding businessmen."

"What about the others, the organized crime I've heard about? Surely they could have followed Bascom here. You arrived with a caravan! You weren't exactly subtle. And how well did you know all the men who helped drive the pieces out here anyway?" Ellie knew she desperately grasped for straws, but she had to. She couldn't wrap her mind around the thought of the gentle man that had befriended her and the others around them as a malicious criminal—or murderer. Especially a murderer of his own family.

"There were those in organized crime, but their goal was to chase the competition out. What would they have to gain by following us way out here? The area isn't that developed."

"Well, the area is apparently developed enough if I have a man coming to my doorstep with an offer of protection that bordered on extortion. He also threatened me. Bascom wasn't that man."

Sheldon nodded as he thought about her words. "True."

"Is this a coincidence?" She pinned him with her glare. "Surely not."

"I don't have the answers you're looking for, Ellie. I wish I did. What I can do is keep my eyes open and try to see that nothing else happens." He pushed away from the rail and prepared to leave. "If you'd like, I can discreetly order a copy of the newspaper that told of the other fire and Bascom's interrogation. Maybe something in there will help you decide whether or not to trust the man you hired."

Ellie hated herself for it, but she nodded her agreement. She doubted the paper would arrive in time to do them any good, but it was worth a try. The man before her spoke of Bascom as a good boss, yet in a way Sheldon seemed very eager to have her distrust his employer. She wanted to trust Bascom, but now she didn't know if she could. Did Sheldon have her best interests in mind? Or did he have ulterior motives for wanting her to dislike Bascom? Perhaps it was something as simple as rivalry for her interest. There weren't many available females out this way, and both men seemed lonely and in want of her attention.

eight

Bascom half listened to Priscilla's chatter as he studied Ellie's mannerisms. Every movement of her body screamed discomfort, but she'd assured him through a strained smile that everything was fine. Still, she'd definitely been distant the past few days.

"Mr. Anthony, are you listening to me?" Prissy danced beside them as they walked. "I'm telling you something very important, and you're staring and staring at my mama."

Bascom felt his face flame as Ellie turned to scrutinize him with a stare.

"It isn't polite to stare, you know. My grammy tells me that all the time. I mostly only stare at people at the dinner table, but only if they're funny looking." Priscilla tilted her head and stared at her mother. "Do you think my mama is funny looking?"

"Prissy!" Ellie admonished. "That isn't something you ask a person."

The child's face crinkled into a look of genuine confusion, and Bascom had to bite back his smile. "I don't find your mother funny looking at all. As a matter of fact, I find her to be quite beautiful, just like you."

"You do?" Now a sly smile replaced her frown. "You could marry us. We need a husband around here."

Ellie gasped audibly. "Priscilla Anne Weathers! You stop that kind of talk this instant. You know better."

"But it's true! The other husband that lived here died when I was too little to remember him, and now I don't have a

69

daddy. Bascom's a nice man."

"Young lady, if you don't hush right now, we'll turn around this moment and return to the house, where you'll spend your afternoon in your room."

"You mean *our* room. Miss Wanda took your room. Mary Ellen Marchison told me that if you married Mr. Anthony, you could sleep back in your room with him and I could have my room back." Apparently mistaking her mother's speechless mortification for hurt feelings, she hurried on. "I like sharing a room with you. You're very warm to snuggle with. But now Mary Ellen and I can't play in there because all your things crowd my things. And Mr. Anthony would probably like to snuggle with you, too, so you wouldn't be lonely."

Bascom grinned. He didn't realize a person's face could turn so many shades of mottled purple and red at one time. Ellie refused to acknowledge Bascom's amused perusal.

Her voice grated out from between her clenched teeth. "Young lady, turn around and march your little body back to the house at once."

Still completely unaware of her mother's chagrin, Priscilla stared at her a moment. "If we return home, we won't get a chance to look for the North Shore Monster."

Indecision battled across Ellie's features. "Then that's a decision you'll have to make. By continuing your stream of completely unacceptable questions to Mr. Anthony, you'll make the choice to finish our walk right now."

Bascom decided to rescue them both. He could see their similarities didn't end with their looks. Stubbornness seemed to run a close second, and at this point both ladies had dug their heels into the ground and the line was drawn. He understood Ellie's need to corral her young daughter and discipline her for disrespect, but if that were to happen, their walk would end prematurely, and Bascom wasn't ready for it to be over. He needed to find out what caused the original distress in Ellie's countenance.

"What's the North Shore Monster?" He feigned fear, looking all around them.

Prissy giggled, and the moment of tension passed. "It won't hurt you. It lives in the water."

Bascom glanced at the lake. "It lives in the water where I swim?"

"Yes."

"Then perhaps I'll continue to walk when I feel a need to stretch my muscles. Our swim excursions will have to end."

The young girl looked horrified.

"Perhaps you should tell me about him. Maybe I'll change my mind."

"Like my mama just did when I talked about the..."

"Prissy!" Ellie warned with a hiss.

"Sorry. Well, he's called the North Shore Monster and—"

"Wait a minute."

Prissy scowled at Bascom's interruption. "What?"

"This is the south shore."

She glanced up at her mother and registered Ellie's nod before she returned her gaze to him. "Right."

"Shouldn't we be looking for the South Shore Monster, then?"

Rolling her eyes, Prissy let out a breath of exasperation. "No. There isn't a South Shore Monster. It's only the North Shore Monster."

"Hmm." Bascom offered Prissy his elbow, which she delightedly clasped with her small hand, which allowed Ellie to tread alongside and gather her frazzled nerves. "Tell me more."

"He's large, with the body of a croc'dile and a head like a horse. Some men saw him when he chased them, and they had to run away and hide until morning!"

"Indeed?" Bascom surveyed the water once more before easing her in the direction away from shore. "Did this happen today?"

Priscilla laughed the deep belly laugh he loved to hear and in return pushed him back toward shore. "No. It happened weeks and weeks ago." She released her hold on his arm and ran ahead.

Ellie quietly snickered.

Bascom glanced at her with raised eyebrows.

"It was sighted mid-1877," she whispered, amusement written all over her face. "So more like years and years ago. Eighteen to be exact."

"I see." He knew his own eyes mirrored the humor sparkling in hers. Relieved that she regrouped so quickly, he also noticed she'd lost the earlier distance she'd put between them. "Has this monster been sighted since?"

She shook her head no. "Rumor has it the creature they saw is nothing more than a buffalo."

"Mr. Bascom Anthony!" Prissy bellowed. "C'mere!"

She crooked her finger his way. He walked over to her and bent close. "Someone else saw it, but they said it looked like a dolphin out by that island." She pointed. He saw a landmass opposite them across the lake.

"So, much closer in our direction." He acknowledged her comment with raised eyebrows.

Ellie caught up to them. "Yes, but that sighting was over thirty years ago. So if that's the case, the North Shore Monster, if they were one and the same, moved north from here, not the other way around."

"Oh, Mama," Priscilla pouted. "If he moved north from here. . .can't he move back to the south? Doesn't the north water touch the south water, too?"

"I suppose it's all one and the same." Ellie lifted her petite shoulder and shrugged in defeat.

"She has a good mind." Bascom watched the little girl run ahead again.

"That she does." She matched her steps to his as they followed along after the lively child. "She must get that from our original husband."

He glanced over, worried that she'd go into her dour mood again, but only saw laughter in her expression.

"I'm sorry if she embarrassed you or put you in an awkward position. I honestly don't know where she gets such ideas. Sometimes she wears me out with her constant questions and fast-thinking responses."

They walked in silence for a few minutes.

"And I suppose she might even be right. If we had a husband around as she says, a lot of things would be easier. We wouldn't be such an easy target for the arsonist or the man that wants me to pay him off for protection. We'd have our own."

Her voice drifted off, and he didn't know what to say.

She hugged her arms around her midsection, an action both defensive and lonely. He wished he could give her the security she needed. Perhaps this was why she'd been so distant and quiet earlier.

He chuckled. "I'm not sure if you're proposing to me or just speaking your thoughts aloud."

She whipped her head his way, her hands flying up to cup her cheeks, this time blushing to her ears. "Oh goodness, no! Maybe Priscilla does get a touch of her precociousness from me. I didn't mean anything. . . . I . . ."

He waved her words away. "I'm only kidding. I wanted to see a smile reappear on your face. You've looked much too serious for most of this walk. If my company upsets you so or causes you concern, I can walk the other direction next time."

Her eyes widened before she looked away, a sure sign of guilt. Surely she didn't mistrust him! He had no idea why she'd feel that way. He considered her reaction. More than likely he'd only hit close to the truth with his words. She did have concerns, but as his hostess, she didn't feel she could burden him with them. The man's visit to coerce money for protection must have shaken her up more than she let on. Then, with the fire on top of his visit, she had reason to worry.

Bascom couldn't do a lot, but he could definitely patrol the resort's grounds during the night. Wanda had mentioned in passing that the early season had been slow to start, and he was sure Ellie didn't have the budget to hire security. Perhaps he and Sheldon could take turns standing watch. He dismissed that idea as soon as he had it. For some reason, he felt the need that he alone should watch out for and defend the four females and their guests. He'd begin his patrols that very night.

❧

Ellie finished the evening's Bible reading and Whimsy tale and lifted the sleepy Priscilla into her arms. Her grandmother had nodded off over her knitting sometime during the Bible story. She'd tuck her daughter in and then return to assist the elderly woman to her bed.

Prissy didn't budge as Ellie lifted the comforter over her sleeping form. The moonlight shone in through the open window, and a cool breeze blew into the room. Ellie considered closing the window, but if she did, the room would become too hot. She shook off her apprehensions and hurried out the bedroom door.

"Gram," she said after returning to the parlor. She gently shook the older woman's arm. "It's time for bed. Let me help you to your room."

Her grandmother abruptly roused from her slumber. "Nonsense, Ellie Lyn. I won't have you tucking me in like a little child. I'm perfectly capable of getting myself to my chamber."

"Yes, ma'am." Ellie bit back her grin and helped her grandmother to her feet. She carefully put the knitting needles and yarn into the basket beside the rocker as her grandmother shuffled away.

Ellie cringed as the older woman reached for the wall, using it to aid her balance and offer support. Support that Ellie was more than happy to give. Stubbornness apparently ran through more than two generations in the family.

"Everyone tucked away for the night?" Wanda entered the parlor from the kitchen. "I finished the dishes from dinner and prepared for tomorrow's morning meal. We should have a few more guests than usual. Things are picking up again."

"They are. I've noticed. Besides our regulars, the supply wagon has dropped off letters of request from new customers, too." Ellie wrapped her arms around herself and stood at the window, peering out into the dark. The moon grew bigger every night but didn't cast much light on the land between the house and lake. The wind picked up, and a gust blew in and knocked over several pictures that had rested on the small round table in front of the window.

Wanda and Ellie both reached for and stabilized them before they could fall to the floor.

"I'd best close this window before the furniture starts to move!" Ellie joked. The winds that blew over the water could be extreme at times, especially during storms.

"You do that. I'm going to settle here and try to catch up on my reading. That is"—she peeked over the top of her glasses—"unless you have something more for me to do?"

"No, there's nothing at all. You rest here. I'm going to go onto the porch and sit outside the door until the wind chills me or blows me back inside."

"I don't blame you. It's a beautiful night right now. Enjoy it while you can. Storm'll be here before you know it."

Ellie wandered outside, knowing she was safe with Wanda's presence on the other side of the wall. She sat in her favorite chair and looked out over the water. The sky had darkened where the storm clouds gathered. It would be a cozy night. Her thoughts, as usual, drifted to Bascom, and she wondered if he'd turned in early.

As soon as she had the thought, she saw a dark figure slip around the far side of the house. All the guests had retired for the night and were safely ensconced in their rooms. She didn't want to wake any of them, but the intruder had headed in the direction of the pavilion. If she took time to alert Bascom, she'd lose sight of the person. If she didn't follow him now, it might be too late. She knew it wasn't the smartest thing to do, but it would only take a scream to wake everyone at the resort. Without a further thought for her safety, she slipped from the porch and followed the dim figure around the building.

She walked as quietly as possible and stepped into the darkness at the side of the house. A strong hand grabbed her arm and pulled her close against the intruder's chest. As she started to scream, a hand clamped across her mouth. The inappropriate thought that her captor smelled nice crossed her mind. And she had to admit, if she was going to meet her demise, she'd rather it be the most pleasant experience it could be. She'd rather her dying breaths not be filled with a strange man's bad body odor or sweat.

"Ellie Lyn, what are you doing out here at night like this? What if someone else had grabbed you instead of me?"

"Bascom?" His use of her grandmother's personal endearment for her didn't slip past her notice. "I could ask you the same thing. Why are you skulking about my resort in the dead of night? You didn't even come up to the porch to chat with me."

She realized he still held her close in his embrace. His rapid heartbeat sounded against her ear, and she wanted to hold tight and absorb his security and strength. She didn't feel as if she were in any kind of danger.

"I wasn't skulking. I was patrolling."

"Then why not stand out where you can be seen? Wouldn't that make more sense? Once trespassers knew you were here, they'd surely leave."

"Not if they're the ones I dealt with back home."

His words caused a shiver of dread to pass through her, and she pulled away slightly, trying to see his face in the murky light from the cloud-encased moon. "You think they followed you? But why?"

"I don't know for sure. But the fire the other day felt like a warning." He gently set her away from him. "A warning I intend to heed."

She felt adrift now that she was out of his arms. She hadn't been held by another man since Wilson died, and she'd forgotten how wonderfully reassuring a man's strong embrace could feel. But it was improper for them to be out here, unchaperoned in the dark while in each other's arms.

He led her onto the porch and sat her in a chair. The sound of Wanda just inside the door, where she conversed with Sheldon, carried out to them. Bascom settled close beside her, his warm breath caressing her cheek.

"Ellie, where do you stand spiritually?"

Not the words Ellie had expected to hear from him. What she'd hoped he'd say, she didn't know, but words of endearment that followed her line of thought a few moments earlier would have been nice, or probably more practically, words of explanation on why he'd been patrolling her area without talking to her about it.

"I'm concerned about you. I'd leave, but I'm not sure whatever's been put into action would stop with that. I want you to be safe. I don't want to bring you trouble, but if history—my history—is going to repeat itself, I want to know you've made things right with God."

"Bascom, you're scaring me. Maybe we should involve the sheriff."

"And tell him what, that we think all this stuff we can't prove? I've been through this before. I lost my wife and son in a fire, and it tore me up inside. Sometimes I don't want my ankle to heal because as long as it gives me pain, I remember. I wish I could go back and take the pain for them. But I can't. Instead I found Someone who can take my pain away, and only after I turned my life over to Christ did I finally get the courage to move on. I want you to find that same strength and peace."

Ellie stared at him. He had tears in his eyes, and his voice broke as he talked about the details surrounding the loss of his wife and son. She didn't see how someone who cared so much could ever hurt someone he loved. She could sense that Bascom's faith was real. And she knew she wanted to find the same peace and strength for herself. Bascom was right. It was time to set things right with God.

"I need you to help me."

"It's simple, not like some of the traveling preachers make it sound. The Bible is very clear that all we have to do is realize and accept the fact we can't make it through this life and into heaven unless we allow Jesus to have full control of our lives. Ellie, without faith in the fact Jesus is the only way to God, we'll just not make it. I know some folks believe we can work our way there, but the only way is to accept God's gift—His Son!"

Ellie smiled. "I believe and accept. Will you pray with me? I'm not sure what to say."

Relief filled Bascom's eyes as he returned her smile and shifted closer. "I will. Let's pray together right now."

nine

"What is it now?" Ellie didn't want to know, but she had to ask. Bascom and Sheldon stood near the water pump, hats in hands, deep in conversation. During the several days that had passed since Bascom started his nightly patrols, the vandalism had stepped up, and it seemed various events now occurred or were noticed on a regular basis.

Bascom looked at her with somber eyes. "Which incident do you want to hear about first?"

Ellie raised a hand and held it against her rapidly beating heart. "There's more than one today? Why doesn't someone catch the person responsible? I mean. . .I know you've both worked hard to cover the grounds at night. But how is this person getting past you?"

"We have been working hard, but whoever is doing this continues to outwit us." Sheldon's exasperation carried through in his words. "It seems wherever we patrol, the vandals hit us from another angle."

"I know it's not your fault," Ellie hurried to soothe. "The night patrols are over and beyond your carousel duties. I hope you know how much I appreciate you both. I'm just wondering. . ."

"Go ahead," Bascom prompted. "You're wondering. . .what?"

"Maybe it's time I go ahead and hire a security team. No one's going to stay here if we're continually under attack."

"Can you afford it?"

"I'm not sure that's the proper question. Can I afford not to? Word gets around, and while I know we've heard rumblings of similar activities happening at other resorts around the lake, the majority seem to be—or at least feel like—they are happening to us here. I can't afford to lose any of the customers that are expected to arrive for the season. I need to assure them their stay will be pleasant and they will feel safe." She sent Bascom an imploring look as tears of frustration pushed against the corners of her eyes. "And right now, even I don't feel safe."

"None of the attacks have been against a person." Bascom, apparently determined to make her feel better, had hit her main concern on the head.

"Yet. But what if they soon are? I don't feel safe outside at night. How can I expect to let my guests walk the shores of the lake by moonlight? If they were to stumble upon the vandal committing a crime, who knows how either party might react? I sure can't tell them in advance to take caution and not to approach a villain. That would send people running right out the door."

Bascom nodded but didn't say anything. Instead he stared off into the distance for a long moment. "I think you're jumping the gun, but I understand what you're saying."

Ellie uncharacteristically found herself taking in his appearance more than his words. He always looked tidy in the morning, and even when ruffled later in the day with wood shavings clinging to his clothes, he took care to present himself neatly. Today he wore a blue woven shirt that buttoned down the front. His light wool pants would surely snag on the wood chips as he carved. His clothes always carried the fresh aroma of outdoors along with the nose-tingling scent of newly cut wood. His hair shone gold in the early morning light, and when the sun caught his eyes, the brilliant blue sparkled with an inner light. Even now, when stressed, he also wore a sense of security and peace.

She thought about their late-night chat earlier in the week

and his encouragement that she put her focus on living her life as a follower of Jesus. The conversation had kept her awake late during the following nights, but while she knew he spoke from experience, she didn't see how putting her faith in something she couldn't see would help her while dealing with a destructive force she couldn't see. Right now her focus needed to be on finding the person or persons responsible for the attacks on her resort, not on musings of things unseen in the spiritual realm.

"Ellie?" Bascom's question broke through her thoughts.

Just like her focus should be on Bascom's words right now and listening to his idea on how to better protect their establishment. "I'm sorry; I got lost in my thoughts for a moment."

"I'm saying I don't think we need to rush into a decision like hiring a team. Let's take a bit more time and see what happens. Maybe the attacks will slow as the season begins in earnest. If it's a competitor, surely the busyness of life will stop further meddling with us."

Us. He said the word as if he had a vested interest in her place. While on the one hand, she appreciated having a strong man around to give her support in running the resort; on the other hand, she resented having him move into her territory when she'd been doing fine on her own before his arrival.

And though she'd been feeling more at peace about Bascom's presence and her ability to trust him, she again felt the fleeting undercurrent of distrust at his words. Did he discourage her from hiring more protection because he honestly felt up to the task on his own? Or did he discourage her because he didn't want extra interference while trying to carry out the task of ruining her?

But what reason would he have to ruin her? He'd been a stranger before her grandfather hired him to build their carousel. *The carousel. . .* He'd said it was his best yet. Could it be that he became so attached to his creations that even though working for hire, he couldn't bear to leave his work behind in the hands of others?

"How many carousels have you built and sold?" Her question burst forth without thought of the consequences or of how odd she would sound asking such an inane thing in the midst of a crisis.

Bascom let out a small laugh while looking perplexed. "Carousels? Well, I suppose around a dozen or so. Why do you ask?"

"Just wondering." She felt silly. If there were that many then he surely didn't grow abnormally attached to his work. Unless. . . another disturbing thought occurred to her. "Have there been other—incidents—with any of the other attractions? If so, how many?"

A cloud passed over his eyes. Whether from her question or her distrust she didn't know. And at this point, she didn't care. She just wanted answers.

"Well, other than the one that took the lives of my family"—he hesitated and peered into her eyes—"none."

"I see."

"Do you?" His eyes narrowed and a look of hurt passed through them. "Why would you ask?"

"I'm just trying to understand what's going on. The attacks started after your arrival. . ." Her words tapered off as she realized how awful and accusing she sounded. "I'm sorry. I didn't mean. . . I just. . ."

He waved her away, and her heart dropped. She hadn't meant to hurt him. He'd done nothing but help her, and she'd insulted him.

"Bascom, please. Listen. I'm just wondering, could someone be following you, perhaps someone trying to pursue a vendetta?

We've talked about this. Do you think your past is connected with the present vandalism?"

"I've thought long and hard, and there isn't anyone that I know of. But there was the fire that killed my family. That wasn't an accident, so yes, I guess someone could possibly be following me." He stared at her a long moment, disappointment evident in his censuring gaze. He then looked past the resort and toward the water. "I think it's best if I pack up and leave. Sheldon's capable of putting the finishing touches on the carousel."

"No, Bascom. I don't want you to leave. If this is a vendetta against you or a tactic of the competition, your departure isn't going to make it all better. If anything, it will make things worse. I won't have. . ."

She flushed as she realized what she'd almost blurted out. *I won't have your steadfast support and strength beside me.*

"You won't have what?" He sounded tense, ready to move on. Or could he possibly be worried that she'd figured out his plan?

A low growl of frustration escaped her. "I won't have your support, and I've really grown to rely on your presence. I mean, I know you have to leave soon, and we'll be on our own at that time, but—I want you to finish what you started. I want you to be here when the carousel is completed."

"As you wish."

His agreement to stay could have been a bit more heartfelt instead of voiced with frustration, but he had a reason to be upset. She'd attacked his character, insulted him, and disappointed him all in a few choice sentences. She'd read some verses in the Bible somewhere during the last few days about guarding the words that came from your mouth because of their power to hurt. This must be what that teaching referred to. She'd just have to work extra hard to make things up to him and to right her wrong.

"I'm sorry if I offended you. It wasn't my intent. I know we're all testy right now, and you, especially, must be very tired." That didn't come out right, either. Now it sounded as if she blamed him for their stilted conversation, based on his lack of sleep.

This time his eyes twinkled as he took in her dismay. "Apology accepted. Would you like to see the damage now? Or would you prefer we just deal with it?" He motioned between himself and Sheldon, who had become silent during their exchange.

"I'd like to know, please." She stepped closer, surveying the pump to the well. The handle lay on the ground, the connector smashed beyond use. "Oh. We can't fix this, can we? It won't fit back on, and even if it did, there's no way to secure it." Without the pump handle, they couldn't access their water. Ellie felt overwhelmed with despair. Why were these things happening to her? She fought the tears that again threatened to overfill her eyes.

"Aw, c'mon, Mrs. Weathers," Sheldon reached over and awkwardly patted her upper arm. "We'll get this thing going again. It won't be a problem for us at all."

Bascom nodded. "We have everything we need in the pavilion. This will be a breeze. The other thing we need to show you is a bit more problematic."

He led her to the side of the pavilion, the main side her guests would see, and she saw the huge splatter of white paint that ran down the wall to the ground. "Someone had to use a full bucket to do this. Why?" Her voice was a frustrated squeak as she studied the mess. Since it had already dried, washing it off wasn't an option.

"We tried to clean it, but the hardest scrubbing didn't do a thing. It's there for good." Bascom watched her reaction.

She pulled herself together. She wouldn't fall apart in front of these men. "Well then, that does leave us in a predicament, doesn't it?" She lifted her long blue skirt by grabbing two handfuls of material and strode closer to study the wall. After a moment of thought, she again lifted the heavy layers of material and paced back the other way, stopping some fifteen feet away from the offensive wall. "I have a solution."

"What's that?" Bascom voiced the question, though both men looked at her with amusement.

"We'll paint the entire wall white." Her enthusiasm grew as she spoke. "This is actually a blessing in disguise. Look at the building with fresh eyes. It's worn and the wood is tired. A fresh coat of white paint is just the ticket to brighten the place up and make it appear more festive."

Sheldon whistled through his teeth as Bascom laughed. He walked over and grasped Ellie by the waist, swinging her in a circle. "Why, I do believe that's just what this old building needs. You're right."

He set her down, and for a moment she thought he planned to kiss her. Regardless of Sheldon or anyone else that might be watching, she hoped he'd do just that. Instead, he caressed her cheek with his work-worn hand and walked over to peruse the structure. "We'll need to get to it right away. Are you thinking a full coat of paint? Or would you prefer we try to whitewash over the area and do the entire building that way? I think we might be able to scrape away enough paint that the whitewash would cover it well."

"I don't want you two to go to any trouble at all. I'll buy paint in town, and I'll take care of painting it."

"Nonsense. This isn't an easy job."

"You think I'm not up to it?" Her question held a challenge, but she kept her tone teasing.

"I absolutely think you're up to it, but you have a lot to do to prepare for the season. Sheldon and I can do this between rounds of paint on the carousel characters inside. . ."

Ellie glanced at him as his voice tapered off. "What is it?"

"I just realized something. Wait here a minute, will you?"

She nodded and looked at Sheldon, who shrugged.

Bascom disappeared into the building. When he reappeared, he blanched. "Whoever did this used paint meant for the horses and creatures of the carousel."

Ellie could feel the color leach out of her skin. "Did they destroy your work?"

"No, but I'm surprised they didn't. I think I'll take to sleeping out here from now on just to be sure they don't reconsider and try that in the future. Something like that would be devastating."

"Yes, I suppose it would be."

Sheldon motioned toward the pavilion. "I can move from my room out into the pavilion, Bascom. There's no need for you to uproot your living quarters for this. Or I can sleep with my door open. I'd hear anything that went on out here. And whoever is doing this would surely need to light a lamp, so I'd see them before they saw me." He paused. "As a matter of fact, I'd guess my presence is what prevented them from damaging our work in the first place. They must have come in for the paint, heard me rustling around, and instead turned their attention to the outside wall."

"Perhaps. But all the same, I'd feel better, I think, sleeping out here for now."

"What about the ladies?"

"What about them?" Bascom looked at his partner.

Ellie watched the interchange with interest.

"Who will watch over them if we're both out here? What if another fire is set, but this time in the house?"

"I hadn't thought of that." Bascom rubbed his chin with

his thumb while he considered his options. "I suppose you're right. It would be best for me to remain where I am. But you'll need to be extra diligent out here." He sighed. "I wish we could do more."

"For now I think this is all we'll need," Ellie hurried to soothe. "I do appreciate what both of you are doing. If necessary, Wanda and I could take turns with the watches, too."

"Absolutely not."

Ellie startled when both men answered at once. One thing for certain, the men didn't want the ladies interfering with their plans.

She went to bed that night as conflicted as she'd awakened. Distrust and suspicion for both of the carousel designers battled for her desire to believe in them. Alternating between the emotions wore her out. Both men seemed to be in the vicinity of vandalism each time, but only after the fact. Why did they miss the culprit? Was the person that good? Or were they working together for a more sinister reason? Maybe they were partners in crime and thrived on the power to make innocent people cringe with fear. The thought didn't go along with the character of the men she'd come to know.

Since she'd been reading the Bible every night and trying to trust God with her daily life, she decided to trust God with her confusion. She addressed her fears through prayer and asked God to direct her on whom to trust. Peace descended upon her, and she fell into a deep sleep.

ten

"Bascom, could you please stop the wagon for a moment while I speak with my neighbor, Miss Adams?" Ellie placed her hand briefly on her escort's arm, and he urged the horses to the side of the dirt road.

Her elderly neighbor worked in a flower garden alongside the white fence that defined the front of her property. While the small two-story house sat within sight of the resort, they didn't often have a chance to talk.

"Why, Ellie Weathers, it's so good to see you! What brings you out this way?"

"It's good to see you, too." Ellie hid a smile at the woman's playful hat. Her round straw sun hat sported a huge bluebird upon the brim while long black ribbons held it firmly in place under her chin. Considering the fact that the sun lay low on the horizon, there wasn't any need for such a contraption, but people from far and near knew about Miss Adams and her love of hats. "I like your bonnet. It's very pretty."

Miss Adams flushed with pleasure and pushed it back a bit from her face. "Why thank you, dear. It's a gift from a couple that stays here often." A cloud passed across her features.

"What is it?" Ellie hurried to step down from the wagon, concerned that by the sudden change in expression the woman might be ill.

"I'm sure it's nothing. . .but the other day when they were here, they said they saw someone creeping around in the dark. I'm sure there's a reasonable explanation."

Ellie sent a quick glance to Bascom but stopped herself

short of telling the neighbor that they, too, had suspicious events of late. Nothing new had happened since the paint incident earlier in the week. There was no need to worry her when Ellie felt sure the events at their place were personal and directed at someone on the property. If a guest of Miss Adams had seen someone, surely it was because the guilty party had trespassed across her property to get to Ellie's place. She skillfully redirected the conversation. "Miss Adams, I'd like you to meet my escort for the evening, Bascom Anthony. And of course you remember Wanda." She motioned to Wanda on the far side of the seat. "And up ahead, waiting on the horse, is another guest at the resort, Sheldon. We're heading over to Saltair for the evening."

Ellie had an ulterior motive for leaving with both men. In a way she hoped something would happen at the resort while they were gone—nothing that would harm her grandmother or daughter, of course—but anything that would clear her suspicions of Bascom. Just to be on the safe side, she'd informed the retired sheriff that happened to be staying with them for the week of her concerns. She promised him a free night's lodging if he'd watch out for anything suspicious. He assured her he would sit up late with her grandmother and keep on eye on things. Only that knowledge had given her peace on leaving for such a long evening.

His wife had pulled Ellie aside and thanked her for both giving her husband a chance to relive his "glory days" and for allowing her a quiet evening to read and catch up on correspondence. They were a quaint couple, and Ellie hoped they'd come around more in the future. They'd even discussed them staying on permanently, due to the recent events, for free room and board in exchange for the sheriff's security, a notion which gave Ellie tremendous peace. Ellie left her grandmother and Priscilla in the parlor with the couple, and the small girl sat enthralled with the sheriff's stories from his past. Priscilla surely wouldn't miss her Whimsy tale on this special night.

Miss Adams's voice brought Ellie out of her musings.

"You young people have a good time. Hurry on now; don't let me slow your plans." She dusted her hands against her faded blue skirt, leaving a streak of dirt, and bent down to her work.

Bascom helped Ellie back onto the seat before climbing up to sit beside her. They had a tight squeeze on the single bench, but the air around them felt balmy and a nice breeze kept them cool, so no one seemed to mind the arrangement. And if truth be told, Ellie liked sitting so close to Bascom and absorbing his strength when her arm brushed against his.

Bascom and Sheldon had invited all the ladies to accompany them to dinner at the infamous resort, but her grandmother had begged off, insisting she stay back to feed their guests. Prissy, enthralled with her new sheriff friend, surprised Ellie by asking to stay, too. The excursion didn't happen often, and Ellie found herself looking forward to the trip with anticipation. She enjoyed the place, but only for a brief visit. The larger resort had activity all around, and that came with a lot of noise. Though she found Saltair to be very beautiful, she preferred their quiet, much smaller, much cozier place.

Ellie had an awful time getting ready, first trying to decide on suitable attire and then styling her hair. She finally chastised herself for worrying so over her appearance and quickly twisted her hair into a stylish knot at the nape of her neck.

The entire time she dressed, her thoughts had drifted to Bascom. What would he think of her hair? Would he think her elegant or pompous? Would he like the long pink skirt and the way she paired it with the tailored cream blouse she'd chosen to wear? Would it be too dressy or too casual? And why on earth did she care what Bascom thought anyway? She'd pushed the bothersome thoughts aside and hurried out to the parlor. Now they rode in silence, all lost in separate thoughts. Was it a coincidence that Miss Adams's guest saw someone lurking around? Had the person meant harm, but instead took off after seeing the guest in the window?

"Bascom, you heard her. . . . What do you think?"

"About the trespasser?" Bascom asked. "I think it's disturbing in light of what we've experienced, but with no harm done, I don't think she's in any danger."

They rode a bit farther. Saltair appeared on the far horizon.

He cleared his throat. "Her place is tiny. Does she rent rooms? She mentioned a guest."

"She has a small boardinghouse, yes. But she's never had a bit of trouble to my knowledge. She's the sweetest lady you'll ever meet. . .next to my grandmother." She grinned. "It's interesting, though. You put the two of them together, and you've never heard such loud, boisterous females."

He laughed and hurried the horses onward. He nodded toward Saltair. "Tell me about this place."

The resort loomed ahead, big and beautiful.

"Most people come from Salt Lake City by train. As you know, the owners planned it to be 'The Coney Island of the West.'"

At this comment, Bascom's face tightened, and he pressed his lips together in a frown.

"Did I say something wrong?"

"No. It's just that the reference to Coney Island doesn't bring back the most pleasant of memories for me. Remember, that's where the original attacks and fire broke out. It just feels rather ironic. Maybe it's a little too much like Coney in my experience."

"Hmm. I hadn't thought of that. Do you want to change the plans? We can turn around and go home if you'd like."

Ellie felt Wanda take in a deep breath in anticipation of his answer. When he shook his head no, her friend released her breath in a quiet *whoosh*.

"Anyway, they brought in a famous designer, Richard Kletting. His plan called for large posts to be driven into the bottom of the lake as the foundation. The lake has about a foot of sand on top of sodium sulfate. Engineers decided they could force steam down steel pipes to loosen the sodium sulfate compound. They put the posts into place, and after a few hours it hardened again and made the posts virtually immoveable. We've had some huge storms out this way with high winds, and no matter what damage the rest of the place sustains, the resort itself has remained solid."

She glanced from the resort toward Bascom. He stared at her in surprise.

She felt a blush flood through her features. "My grandfather had a certain fascination with the place. He read every article in the newspaper and often talked about the grandiosity of the resort. I'm guessing that fascination had something to do with his 'surprise' of the carousel."

Wanda laughed. "To say he was fascinated is an understatement. I think even Prissy could pronounce *sodium sulfate* as one of her first phrases."

"It is pretty amazing, you have to admit. There aren't many structures such as this around here."

By now they'd neared the monstrosity, and Bascom whistled through his teeth. "I can see why he was impressed. How long did it take to build?"

"Less than a year."

The structure stood several stories high with several towers topped with domes surrounding the various sides. Ornate trelliswork finished out the trim.

They found a place to leave the wagon, and Sheldon tied his horse nearby. They joined the throngs of people entering the arched doorway. Wanda and Sheldon quickly disappeared into the crowd, and Bascom firmly gripped Ellie's arm to prevent her from doing the same.

He leaned close. "Do you want to try and find them? Or would you prefer to head outside onto the boardwalk?"

Ellie motioned for him to continue on through the large building and out the far door. He led her up to the second level, where they stood near the rail overlooking the water. Sunset wasn't far off.

"I'm glad you chose a spot away from the train terminal." Ellie didn't think her nerves could handle the constant noise of the trains that came and went at steady intervals. She could see people dancing inside the large hall behind them.

"It's not quite the atmosphere I envisioned." Bascom's voice, full of remorse, came from nearby. He leaned in so he could be heard. "I thought we'd have a nice, quiet dinner where you could forget about your worries for a night. Instead, it's noisy and not the least bit relaxing."

"Oh, I don't know. I enjoy the excitement. Though I admit I prefer the quiet of our resort for the most part."

Another couple joined them at the rail, overlooking the swimmers in the lake below.

"Ellie?"

Ellie looked over to see another neighbor beside them. "Good evening, Delores. Hank." She introduced Bascom. "It seems to be the night for resort owners here at Saltair."

The couple exchanged a troubled look.

"We didn't leave our resort for the evening without giving it a lot of thought," Hank supplied. "I'm still not sure it was the best idea to come here."

A chill ran down Ellie's back. She had a feeling she knew what her neighbor would say next.

"We've had some. . .occurrences at our place and were hesitant to leave for an evening. Have you noticed anything peculiar over your way?" Hank's blue eyes connected with hers as he waited for a reply.

"We've had a fire and a few pranks pulled around our place. I'm sure it's an unruly neighbor boy or two out for a good time." She didn't know why she added that last part, since the thought had never entered her mind before now. Perhaps denial or wishful thinking had caused the spontaneous words.

"I'm not so sure," Hank continued. "I've talked with the others, and we've all been having some hindrances to our businesses."

Ellie asked the date when his vandalism began and had to mask her concern when she realized the date lined up with Bascom's arrival.

"Well, we'll leave you and your beau to your evening." Delores waved, and the couple continued walking down the wooden planks.

Bascom stared out over the water. Though the sun had begun its descent, neither one spoke of the splendor. Ellie watched the colors filter through wispy clouds. Blue, pink, orange, and finally deep purple as darkness began to fall.

"I can imagine what you're thinking." Bascom's voice, even with the din around them, sounded strained. "This has all followed us here. Whatever is going on seems to be caused by our arrival."

Ellie placed a hand on his arm, trying to gain a bit of warmth as her body shivered in apprehension. For the first time, though, the apprehension dimmed in Bascom's presence. Ellie sent up a silent prayer for discernment and then determined to enjoy their evening.

"Not necessarily. It could all be an awful coincidence. Let's not worry about this for now and enjoy the moment instead."

Bascom agreed and led her to a quieter table overlooking the water. Most swimmers had come ashore, but there were still enough people out there to make their dinner entertaining.

"The water seems shallow here." Bascom bit into a roll.

Ellie nodded. "It is. There's rumor of the water receding enough to put the resort in jeopardy. If it does, the swimmers will be far from the water's edge with a field of mud between them and the water. And the stench and flying bugs won't make visiting here pleasant."

Bascom made a face. "I hope for their sake that doesn't happen. It's a beautiful place."

"It is. And I agree. I'm fortunate that a dry season won't affect us in the same way. Our location is on deeper water."

The sun had set completely and small lanterns lit the tables. The moon shone down on the water, illuminating a path across its surface. Ellie looked in the direction of their place. She couldn't see it from this distance, but suddenly the desire to be on her own quiet porch with only Bascom for company overran the desire to stay in the beautiful but noisy place.

Bascom seemed to read her thoughts. "Shall we find our travel companions and head back home?"

Ellie nodded and allowed him to assist her to her feet. The dinner and company had been wonderful, but the noise and chaos were grinding on her nerves. She spotted her friend across the dining area, and Wanda also stood to her feet. She motioned toward the front of the building, and Ellie nodded. She followed her dapper companion and wished again that the situation were different. Bascom possessed all the attributes she'd want in a father for Priscilla. And in a husband for herself. She brushed away the fanciful musings. Apparently her lack of a Whimsy tale for the evening had her imagination racing in directions where it didn't need to tread. Along with Bascom's arrival came too many questions that remained without answer. And only time would tell if the questions would be answered in a way that she found pleasing.

eleven

"You seemed very relaxed in Bascom's company last night." Wanda handed the last breakfast plate over to Ellie, and Ellie began to wipe it dry. "Did you have a good time?"

"I did. . .and I didn't. Wanda, I'm so confused!" Ellie tossed the dish towel on the counter and settled into a kitchen chair.

Wanda hurried to pour them each a cup of coffee before joining her. "What did I miss? The rides there and home were both pleasant. Bascom seemed to be a model gentleman and escort. . ." Her eyebrows furrowed. "Or was he? Did something happen after we were separated?"

"Oh no, nothing like that." Ellie hurried to wave her concerns away. "Bascom only acted in the most proper of ways. I enjoyed his company."

"Then what? I don't understand."

"I don't either—that's just the problem! I really have grown to enjoy his company. I love our evenings on the front porch when we discuss so many topics. He's very educated."

Wanda placed her hand upon Ellie's. "As are you. I'm sure he's found great pleasure in realizing a woman can carry on such intriguing conversations about so many topics. Your grandfather did you a favor by drawing you in to so many deep talks."

"Indeed, he did at that." Ellie smiled, the memory of their many discussions a fond one. "And I do believe this is part of what draws me to Bascom, now that you mention it. He reminds me a lot of my grandfather."

"He's very handsome."

"Yes. Very." Ellie ran her finger back and forth across the side of her mug. "I love the way his hair flips down across his forehead, partially hiding his eyes. It makes him appear shy. Yet his eyes, they watch every move and miss nothing. His intelligence is mirrored in them. And then there's his one dimple when he does that crooked smile. It makes him appear very gentle and sweet."

"Just to name a few things." Wanda smirked.

Ellie realized she'd been sitting there for several moments, staring off into space with a ridiculous grin on her face. "Wherever is my head today? I need to check on the new reservations, make sure the books are up-to-date, clean the rooms of departing guests. See? He has me all in a dither— yet I can't even trust him. How can I make good choices if my emotions are all tangled up when it comes to Bascom? All my grandfather's training, his trust; I can't betray him now. Nor can I properly raise my daughter if I let a man I barely know throw me into such turmoil."

"I'm afraid I don't understand." Wanda looked genuinely perplexed. "You think he's handsome. He's kind and considerate. He's intelligent. You've known him about six weeks now and have had nothing but exemplary behavior from him. And that makes you a poor judge of character?"

"No, but all the events since his arrival point to his involvement in some way. I can't let my heart rule my common sense. You heard what Miss Adams said about a person in her yard. . . ."

"Who could have been anyone, not necessarily someone up to no good."

"And then we ran into Delores and Hank. They stated they've had some 'hindrances' along with other neighbors."

"He didn't mention what those 'hindrances' were? That could mean anything."

"Well, they were bad enough occurrences that he said it took a lot of thought to get them away for the evening."

"Hmm." Wanda stood and walked to the window.

Ellie leaned back in her chair and crossed her arms, waiting for Wanda to share her thoughts. She'd always trusted her friend and knew she had good insight into such things.

"He's a good man, Ellie. I just know it. He's kind and truly loves the Lord. I don't think you can show that type of devotion without meaning it with the heart. I've heard bits and pieces of the talks you two have shared while out on the porch, and I've had my own conversations with him on the subject. He's very strong in his faith, and it's important to him that those in his path also hear the truth. What reason would he have for deception with such a thing?"

"Oh, I don't know." Ellie joined Wanda at the window and looked out. Dark storm clouds again lingered on the far horizon to the west. The wind had picked up and now blew an old rag across the open expanse between the house and pavilion, plastering it against the porch. "Maybe, if he's a trickster, he just enjoys toying with a trusting female."

"I don't think his personality shows any indication of that at all. . .and I don't think you believe it deep down, either." Wanda turned to face Ellie, and Ellie wrapped her arms around her middle in a defensive gesture. "What I do think is that you've been alone for a long time. I think you feel something for this man and something—guilt? fear?—is gnawing at you and building a protective covering around your heart. Look at you, hugging yourself as if you can protect your heart even now from being broken."

Ellie deflated, relaxing her arms and releasing her tight hold. What silly notions her friend had. As if her embrace could protect her heart from being broken. "You know me too well."

"I know you as all good friends should know each other. Ellie, don't let your fear cause you to miss out on a special man. I know you've begun a relationship with Jesus over the past few weeks. Let Him guide you and pay attention to what's going on around you, but don't push Bascom away and ruin this chance."

"Speaking of, how did *your* evening go with Sheldon?" Ellie decided if she couldn't win the conversation, she could at least divert it. After all, as Wanda had said, she'd learned from the best—her papa.

"My evening didn't go nearly as well as yours. Sheldon is a gentleman, but I had the feeling he only spirited me away in order to allow you and Bascom your privacy."

Ellie felt the blush rise up in her face. "You mean you think they planned it?"

"No, I don't think *they* planned anything. I think this was entirely Sheldon's idea. He forced me right into the heart of the crowd, and we were carried along straight out the back door. I saw you divert to the side and motioned for Sheldon to follow, but he only smiled and continued to press me in the other direction. We had a good time, but his heart wasn't in the evening or events. He was a pleasant companion, and he even took me dancing."

"Wanda!"

"I know, but I was curious. We only stayed a few moments. I should know better at my age, but I wanted to experience the feeling of being held in a man's arms while being whisked about on the dance floor."

"At your age. . .you're only a few years older than me!" Ellie teased. "And as for the dancing, how did it feel?"

Wanda sighed. "In all honesty, it felt flat without being held in the arms of a man that I love. I watched the other couples. Their eyes never left each other's face. You could see the love.

I think without that, something lacks in the experience."

Ellie felt like an awful friend. In all the years that they'd been together she'd never once noticed how lonely Wanda was or that she longed for her own romance to sweep her off her feet. "Well, I'll be the first one to pray that you find that man for yourself."

"I appreciate that. And you know I'm content here with you and Priscilla and your grandmother. I can't imagine a better place to live and spend my years."

"Priscilla." Ellie's emotions plummeted again. "I have to consider her in all this. She's becoming too fond of Bascom, and I can't chance her getting hurt. Maybe I should busy her with other tasks and keep her out of his work area for now."

"Nonsense. She adores him. Just as you miss your husband and grandfather, she misses having a man involved in her life. Bascom seems to enjoy her company. We just discussed all this a moment ago. Why take that relationship away from them?"

"Because something isn't right, and I can't figure out what it is. I can't take a risk that my daughter will suffer for my poor decisions." She grasped her skirt, pulled it up from the floor, and stalked across the kitchen. "Why did the damage to our area start just after his arrival?"

"Do you really think Bascom and Sheldon are the only new arrivals in the area? We all run resorts or hotels or boarding-houses. Newcomers are arriving and leaving on a daily basis. The area has grown quite a bit, and with growth comes crime. Surely you remember all the articles from the newspapers your grandfather loved to discuss with you."

Ellie froze in her tracks. "You're right! I haven't thought of any of those articles in some time. Each week he'd read of new crimes that had happened in town. It's only natural that the criminals would find their way out to us eventually."

"Right. There's bad in the world, no matter where you live."

"I suppose we'd do well to secure the place a bit better. And perhaps we even need to consider buying a weapon of our own." She shuddered at the thought. "Though it's highly unlikely I could ever hurt another person, even if he presented a danger to me."

"What if an intruder presented a danger to someone you love?"

Ellie scowled. "I'd use it in a moment."

"Then I agree this is something we should check into."

Ellie threw her arms around Wanda. "Thank you, Wanda, for helping me sort through my jumbled thoughts. I'm going to check on Prissy."

"You're welcome. Anytime." Wanda turned and busied herself with her bread dough. During the course of their conversation, it had risen past the top of the towel-covered bowl.

Ellie hurried out to the central hall.

A loud roll of thunder sounded from the other side of the window. Ellie smiled, knowing that within moments Prissy would catapult herself around the doorframe from their private quarters and into her mother's reassuring arms. When the little girl didn't appear by the time Ellie had reached their shared room, a small pang of worry filled her chest. She pushed open the door. Though Priscilla's dolls sat at the small table her great-grandfather had fashioned a couple years earlier, the silver tea set sat upon it untouched. Each mug held water, so her daughter's tea party had started after breakfast as the little girl had planned, but where was she now?

The laundry room. Prissy found a certain fascination with the steam-powered washing machine and went out to watch it at every chance. Ellie's heart plummeted with relief at the realization. She headed out the door, only to have it wrenched from her hands by the strong wind. The scent of oncoming rain hung heavy in the air, and the clothes on the line whipped furiously in all directions. Ellie wanted to reassure her daughter, but she needed to get the linens down before they were drenched.

Since her daughter hadn't appeared, Ellie could only imagine that the noise in the laundry was so great that the child hadn't heard the thunder. Another loud boom sounded, and Ellie jumped. She spurred herself into action and began to pull down the laundry into her arms. Wanda joined her, her voice lost in the blowing wind.

Ellie's arms were full, so she motioned with her head in the direction of the laundry room. Wanda nodded and continued to pull down bedsheets. Ellie entered the small room and glanced around as she placed her laundry in a woven basket. Her heart skipped a beat when she noticed Prissy's favorite rag doll lying on the ground. She couldn't remember if Prissy had left it there earlier or not. Ellie scooped up the doll and called Priscilla's name.

"Sweetheart, it's Mama. It's all right to come out now. The storm's not yet here, and if we hurry we can get to the house before the rain arrives."

No answer.

Ellie returned to the open door in time to see Wanda hurry into the house. She pulled the laundry door closed behind her and followed suit. Surely Prissy had returned to their quarters, seeking out her mother. But again only a silent empty room greeted her.

A quick peek into their parlor had showed her grandmother's sleeping form without the companionship of her great-granddaughter.

A sob caught in her throat as she entered the kitchen. The reassuring aroma of baking bread swirled around her, totally incongruent with her sentiments at the moment. Never had Prissy strayed from the house alone.

"Wanda!" Ellie tried to tamp down her terror, but the emotion carried through her panicked voice. "I can't find Prissy anywhere!"

"Ellie? Priscilla's fine. She's in the pavilion with the men. She asked to go earlier in the morning, and Sheldon was here topping off his coffee. He offered to take her. I didn't think you'd mind since she's been out there so many times before. And after we had such a pleasant time last night with the men, I didn't think there'd be any harm with the arrangement."

Ellie lashed out in anger. "Well, you obviously didn't think at all. I've said she could be out there with you or with Gram. I've never said you could leave her alone. I trusted you to. . ." Tears choked off her words. They'd just had a conversation about Bascom and her concerns. Not once had her friend mentioned Priscilla at that very moment was in the sole custody of those men. They could finish this conversation at another time. For now she just wanted to go and retrieve her daughter. "She's probably terrified."

She hurried through the door, leaving her devastated friend behind. "Prissy!"

The wind whipped against her as soon as she left the protection of the back of the house. A wall of rain immediately soaked through her clothes. The lake provided a smooth surface for the winds to blast over, and now she had to lean forward to avoid being blown back as she forced her way to her daughter. She prayed the men had the sense to keep the little girl under their care with the storm raging outside. She prayed even harder that the men would indeed be *in* the pavilion with her daughter. What if they'd taken off with her? Maybe Bascom missed his own child so much that he'd decided to take Prissy as his own. "Prissy!"

The pavilion door burst open and slammed back against the wall. Even over the high wind Ellie could hear her daughter's lighthearted and slightly off-tune voice singing along with Sheldon. Ellie didn't notice she'd frozen in her steps with relief until Bascom grasped her arm and pulled her inside. The interior felt cozy after the raging storm outside. But that was nothing compared to the storm of fear raging inside Ellie's heart.

"How dare you take my daughter without my permission? How dare you!" Ellie pummeled her fists against Bascom's chest with anger. Bascom stood there and allowed her to vent her frustrations. He finally pulled her into his embrace, and she cried, "I was so scared. I couldn't find her anywhere."

Sheldon appeared at her side. "I'm so sorry, Ellie. I had no idea. I figured Wanda would tell you I had Prissy out here."

"Well, she didn't." She knew her attitude toward her guests and best friend was inexcusable. But she'd never felt so terrified in her life. She tore herself away from Bascom's solid arms and swiped at her tears. Everything in her life felt like it was falling apart. Everything felt in an upheaval. She reached for her daughter, pulling her tight against her chest. "Oh, baby, let's get back to the house."

"At least wait until the storm abates. It isn't safe to be out there right now." Bascom's worried eyes surveyed her.

"I'm soaking wet and need to get into dry clothes. I'm not leaving my daughter for another moment. And look, I've already drenched her, too."

"Then at least allow me to accompany you back to the house." He snatched an overcoat from a hook on the wall. He gently pried Prissy from Ellie's tight embrace and pulled Ellie up against his side. He draped the coat across her and Priscilla and led them back into the storm and to the house door.

The winds diminished once they were on the back porch and directly out of the brunt of things. Bascom stared at her for a long, silent moment. He passed Prissy back over to her. "I'd never hurt you or your daughter, Ellie. I'm disheartened that you'd even think such a thing. Her safety is both mine and Sheldon's utmost concern when she's out in the pavilion with us."

Ellie opened her mouth to speak, but no words came out against the disappointment in his eyes. He hurried back out into the storm, disregarding the fact that he, too, was now completely soaked. She pulled Priscilla close against her chest and sank back against the wall. She'd have a lot of apologizing to do, but for now she'd get them both into fresh clothes. Only later, after they'd changed, did she realize she'd entered the forbidden pavilion and hadn't even bothered to take note of the carousel's progress.

twelve

Bascom ducked his head against the wind and hurried out into the driving rain. The large drops pelted against his eyes, blinding him as he moved toward the pavilion's door. Once he arrived, he fought to pull it open. The relentless wind fought back. He slipped through the small opening, and the door slammed back into place, barely missing his hand as he snatched it out of the way. He leaned against the door, exhausted, the rough wood hard against his back as he stared across the room. The sizeable attraction loomed in the dusky interior, and for the first time, Bascom felt doubt over a project.

Always before he'd known he'd captured the essence of what the prospective owner envisioned. But in those cases, the person who'd hired him had been either the potential owner and known exactly what he wanted or an overindulgent parent wanting a small carousel horse for a child's gift.

Ellie had resented his presence from the start, and now with the vandalism and unrest that followed soon after his arrival, her resentment moved into distrust. And even with all that aside, even without the interference of the attacks on her place, he just wasn't sure she'd like the creation he'd developed. She saw the purchase as an extravagance they hadn't been able to afford. Bascom had no clue as to her financial status and he, too, questioned whether her elderly grandfather had made a poor choice in purchasing the carousel. But there was no turning back now. No one else would want a merry-go-round with this theme—it was exclusive to Ellie.

He sighed. He'd just have to make it unique enough to

become the draw her grandfather had hoped for. Maybe if she could think of it like that, as a way to honor his final request, it would help with her frustration.

Wandering forward, Bascom looked at the beautiful merry-go-round that filled the room. He caressed the shiny wood of the completed horses. The specialty wood carvings were coming together and would soon be set into place beside the traditional ones.

Bascom slipped out of his dripping overcoat and moved to his favorite design, the mermaid. He ran a hand down the side and felt rough edges. The rote work of smoothing and shaping rough edges into soft curves welcomed him. Working with wood always relaxed him, so he picked up a chisel and started chipping away.

If only he could smooth Ellie's rough edges as easily. A small smile tipped his mouth at the thought. He knew he wouldn't change her even if he could. Her rough edges were also tempered with softness, judging from the warm way she responded to her daughter and to the consideration she gave her grandmother and Wanda.

She easily switched from concern to gracious host. He'd observed that transition several times during their evenings on the porch when he arrived unexpectedly. She'd be lost in thought, staring out over the lake, her forehead furrowed with concentration, but as soon as she registered his arrival, a smile would slip into place and she'd welcome him with cheery warmth.

A quiet chuckle sounded behind Bascom. "You work that mermaid any harder and she'll collapse into sawdust the moment a child sits upon her." Sheldon left the doorway of his private quarters and approached the work area.

Bascom surveyed the piece. "I guess I did get a bit over-zealous for a moment there."

"What were you thinking about? The way you were digging into the surface, it looked like you had a personal vendetta against the poor girl."

More like a vendetta against whoever keeps putting a frown on Ellie's face. Bascom didn't share the sentiment with his friend.

"It's Ellie, isn't it?"

Sheldon straddled a high-back chair and slapped his work gloves against his palm. The noise grated on Bascom's already shredded nerves.

"It's everything." Bascom put down his tool and paced across the hard-packed dirt floor. "It's like Coney Island all over again. I don't understand. It's like a personal vendetta, but I have no known enemies."

"The men responsible are all behind bars, correct?" Sheldon stopped the annoying slap-slap-slapping and held the gloves still, contemplative. "Do you suppose there's a chance that one of them is free or that perhaps one of the captured men had help from someone on the outside who's still on the loose?"

"I have no idea about any of it. I only know that my family paid the price for an attack planned against me, and I won't stand by and watch the same happen to another family."

"What are you saying? Do you want to leave?" Sheldon's eyes narrowed. "I suppose I can handle the finish work. You've taught me well. But I'm not sure that will stop whatever's going on."

Bascom, deflated, sank onto a chair and sat opposite his apprentice. "That's my concern, too. If I left and something happened to any of them, I'd feel even worse. Perhaps by staying I can figure out what's going on and prevent another tragedy."

"Then we need to figure this out together." Now Sheldon paced the length of the pavilion. "Can you think of anyone you might have outbid for a project? Did you ever have a run-in with a competitor that blamed you for getting a contract he wanted?"

"No, nothing. I'm contacted by my clients; I don't go seeking them out. If ever there was a situation like that, I know nothing about it." Bascom thought hard but couldn't come up with a thing he'd ever done to warrant the violence and anger of which he'd been a victim. "I can't even think of a situation where that would be possible. Carousel designers are a small breed. There aren't many of us available. So there's more demand than supply in this case. You know that. Why would anyone care about a contract when there are plenty more for the taking?"

"That's a good point."

Silence pressed in, but nothing new came to Bascom.

"Perhaps. . ." Sheldon hesitated, measured Bascom with a glance, then continued. "Perhaps it's personal."

"What do you mean by that?" Bascom had no idea to what his friend referred. "What kind of personal situation would ever drive a person to commit murder?"

"I can think of quite a few instances. The newspapers are full of stories. Maybe someone courted your wife before you and the fire was his way of lashing out?"

"Not that I know of. Susan only had eyes for me." Bascom shrugged. "And if there ever was anyone else, she never spoke of him."

"Never? Surely she had other suitors. Your wife was a very beautiful woman." Sheldon walked over and stared at the rain running down the window in tiny streams. "Maybe it was someone she toyed and flirted with, someone who thought he meant more to her than he really did?"

"Susan? Not a chance," Bascom snapped. "She didn't have a mean bone in her body, and she had a good sense about her. She'd never lead a man on for the thrill. You knew her better than to ask that."

"Then someone who *thought* she felt that way? Maybe someone mistook her sweetness for interest? She might have been the intended target all along." Sheldon spun around at this new inspiration. "All this time you thought you were the target. You've tortured yourself with the thoughts of what you could have done differently, how you could have saved them, correct?"

"But what else could it be? You agree that Susan didn't have a mean bone in her body. Surely the cruel act against them was intended for me alone."

"In a roundabout way, yes. In this person's eyes, you 'stole' Susan away from him. By his hurting her, you'd be hurt, too. Especially if during the process of an inquisition, a seed of doubt about your reputation could be instilled in everyone around you. And when you think about it, that's exactly what happened."

Bascom thought about his words. Sheldon could be right. If so, Bascom wasn't directly responsible for his family's death as he'd thought. He'd only been a victim of the same crazed person's scheme. But a missing piece didn't make sense. "What about the men put away for the crime?"

Sheldon raised a shoulder. "I don't know, but I guess they were still guilty for the lesser charges. So even if they were honest when they denied the attack against your family, they still deserve to be right where they are."

"That's true. They still stood guilty of setting the other fires at the other establishments and the coercion."

The rain had slowed, and Bascom stood and walked to the window. He saw movement near the porch and even through the blurry window knew Priscilla hopped back and forth across the porch in play. He'd grown to love the child in his short stay and determined again to see things through so that when he moved on, it would be with a clear conscience and the knowledge that all was well with the ladies. "And what of the attacks against the other resorts?"

"The killer could be pacing himself so he doesn't end his quest too quickly. . .or maybe he's just trying to throw off suspicion by not doing all the acts in one place." He walked to the outer door. "The rain's slowed enough that I'm going out for some fresh air. Let me know if you need anything."

Bascom nodded, already slipping away into his thoughts. Sheldon had given him a lot to think about. Things he should have realized long ago. His grief had been so deep that he'd never even considered any other reason for the violence— other than the crime being directly related to his work. All signs had pointed toward arson with the intent to destroy the newest project because of the owners' refusal to pay for protection. Instead of Bascom telling his wife and son to stay home, he'd led them right into the trap.

But what if Sheldon was right? What if a jilted lover—or worse and more likely—someone who thought he had the potential to gain Susan's love took advantage of the already heated situation at Coney and used that as a cover to get even with them all? A shiver of terror rolled down his back. If so, then the person had followed them here—not a hard thing to do with all the wagons and hoopla that surrounded their arrival—and now Bascom's friendship with Ellie had put her and her loved ones right into the path of a lunatic.

He had to figure out a plan. If he went to the authorities, they'd think him insane. He needed more evidence before they'd take him seriously. Or worse, they'd point the finger of blame toward him once again. Since he'd never invited his family to a work site before, they'd scrutinized the case heavily. The fact that no other sites had ever been located at such a wonderful family destination didn't seem to matter to them. With the other suspects behind bars, Bascom alone would be their prime target.

A sardonic laugh slipped over his lips. A target explained exactly what he was. No matter what, whoever had chased them down made him just that. His guilt over another person's pain, his worry of what would happen if he couldn't stop the attacks, his ending up in jail because the authorities blamed him. . .all added up to a situation of vengeance where Bascom couldn't see a way to clear his name. Maybe the original intent was to hurt Susan, but whoever the killer was, he apparently wasn't done with inflicting pain on the people Bascom loved.

Since the authorities weren't a viable alternative, Bascom would have to find his own way to figure out the mess. He considered all his options. Telling Ellie wasn't the best idea since she already distrusted him and blamed him for various things from financial woes to taking advantage of her grandfather while the old man lay in a feeble state. While Bascom had had no way to know of such a thing, Ellie obviously hadn't come to that realization yet. He could do nothing and keep watch, but that went against Bascom's nature. He needed to be a step ahead of the tormentor. Susan and Billy didn't have a chance. They had no warning. This time Bascom did, and not to act on it seemed ridiculous.

His strongest plan would be to spend more time in Ellie's company, hoping any further assaults would force the killer out into the open and into a confrontation. If so, then Bascom, along with Sheldon and any male guests that were around, could hopefully subdue the criminal before further damage was done. He'd finally know his enemy. That's when they could bring in the law. At the very least, Bascom would feel better knowing Ellie rested safely under his care. He would protect her to the best of his ability. He smiled, knowing the rain had been a blessing in disguise. Given the killer's favorite method of attack seemed to be through fire, the wetness of the drenched structures would prolong another round.

Since Ellie had left in a huff and wouldn't necessarily be open to Bascom's company, the opportunities to spend more time together would be harder to come by. But still Bascom determined this angle to be the best remedy for that situation. If Susan were here, she would be the first to attest to the fact that when Bascom turned on the charm, he was hard to resist. She'd said many times over that Bascom had done just that with her, and she'd had no eyes for anyone else from that moment on.

Of course if Susan were there, none of the bad stuff would have happened and he wouldn't be in this mess. If the same reaction rang true with Ellie, Bascom could keep her nearby at all times, under his watchful eye. Daytime hours wouldn't be a problem. There were too many people around, and no attacks that he knew of had been initiated during those hours. Bascom could finish the carousel and ready it for their grand opening. He had some ideas to share with Ellie, and now that he thought of it, that would be the perfect opening into spending more time in her company. She'd consider his words in the name of bettering her resort and its reputation. Now he only had to put his plan into effect.

thirteen

"You still don't trust me."

Ellie froze in place at Bascom's direct words, her hand still resting in the water where she trailed it over the side of their small wooden boat. "That's not tr..."

But she couldn't deny what they both knew to be fact. His words *were* true. She'd avoided all contact with him during the past few days and sat in the boat with him now only because Wanda hadn't given her a chance to refuse Bascom's invitation after lunch.

"I can see it in your eyes, not that you'll look at me very often."

She now raised her eyes to his, sure he could see her regret. His mouth curved into a sardonic half smile, but his blue eyes held no trace of humor. She winced at the hurt that filled them.

"I'll leave if that will make you feel better. Sheldon can finish up the few loose ends and put the final touches on the carousel."

He'd stopped rowing and now rested the oar across his legs. The water dripped off the end of the thin piece of wood, the sound of the droplets as they hit the surface of the lake the only sound to break the silence. From where they sat far from the shore of the lake, they seemed to be the only life around. No one would interrupt the conversation in time to rescue Ellie from responding. If only she'd insisted on bringing Prissy along....

But Ellie knew the talk was a long time coming and overdue. She'd missed Bascom's teasing banter and friendly wave across the open area between the house and pavilion. She'd grown accustomed to their evening chats, and now, ever since she'd lambasted him about Prissy's disappearance days earlier, Bascom hadn't even tried to come around. At first she told herself his lack of presence spoke louder than words about his guilt and that she'd been right in her tirade, but time and Wanda had convinced her of what her heart already knew. Bascom kept his distance out of respect for Ellie and her feelings, not because of any guilt or wrongdoing on his part. Only her stubbornness and lack of a plan on how to fix things kept her from making things right.

"I don't want you to leave." She'd made a mess of things, and she was the one that owed him an apology. And she needed to do so quickly because the thought of Bascom leaving left a queasy feeling in her stomach. "I know you meant no harm to Prissy. . .or to me. She's missed you." Ellie looked away, the intensity in his eyes doing strange things to her stomach. She glanced back and saw that his smile came more naturally. Hope now filled his eyes. "I've, uh, I've. . .missed you. . .too."

For the first time in days his eyes lit up and his mouth quirked into the heart-tugging grin she'd missed. The grin she'd wiped from his face. He leaned toward her and grasped her wrist, tugging her forward toward the seat closest to him. She'd purposefully chosen the farthest seat from his place at the stern. Her heart pounded in her chest as she hesitantly moved forward, clutching the folds of her skirt while balancing carefully in the most central part of the vessel. She stepped over the bench with one leg and swung the other over quickly as the boat rocked, causing her to plop quickly onto her seat.

The silence spread around them, but this time it was a comfortable silence, and she no longer wished for Prissy's presence.

Bascom leaned close, his knees brushing against hers. "I've missed you, too. I've missed our chats. I've missed watching you wave while almost walking into the doorway in distraction over my presence."

Ellie gasped, tugging her hand from his. "Not true!"

Bascom's rich, bubbly laugh filled the air. "It is, too. Last Saturday morning you walked straight into the door in your hurry to get inside and avoid me."

She pushed against his egotistical shoulder. "I tripped into the door when my boot heel stuck in the crack of the floor and held me in place when the rest of me thought I'd continue forward. It had nothing to do with your wave, other than the fact that I didn't pay attention to my steps."

"So you admit my presence causes you a distraction."

"I admit nothing of the sort." She cupped her hands against her flaming cheeks and rested her elbows on her knees to avoid his intense stare, a move which caused her to lean forward and increased Bascom's nearness.

"I'll admit it." Bascom also leaned forward, his forehead almost touching hers. "I'll admit you've caused me distraction from the moment I first laid eyes upon you. You've brought the first sign of joy back into my life since I lost my wife and son. You and Prissy fill a void left inside me. I want to explore that further."

"Bascom!" Ellie didn't know what to make of such bluntness. No man, not even Wilson, had spoken so freely in her presence of his feelings and emotions. She imagined her eyes now reflected her horror and panic at being in such a quandary. She covered them with her hands so he couldn't read the emotions within.

"Ellie." He gently pulled her hands away and forced her to look up at him. "If I've learned one thing, it's that relationships can be fleeting. There's no guarantee of the time one might have with another." He shifted in his seat and repositioned the oar. He worried his lower lip with his teeth and watched her thoughtfully before resuming his speech. "There might not be a second chance if you let something special slip through your fingers. I don't want to live with regrets. Not any more than I already have, anyway. I care for you, Ellie—a lot—and I care for Priscilla. I feel that you sense the same emotions; you're just afraid to acknowledge them."

He was right, but she didn't know how to let go and trust with all the suppositions careening around in her thoughts. She'd grown through her prayer time and her reading of the Word, but what if in this situation she still went by her own emotions and not God's? She didn't trust her spiritual maturity yet. What if she put herself and Prissy into a dangerous situation because of this confusing and tumultuous feeling of love? The realization of the intensity of her feelings toward Bascom surprised her. If she didn't care deeply about him, why would she miss him so much or care what he thought?

"Love?"

She didn't realize she'd whispered the word aloud until Bascom repeated it and a look of confusion passed over his face. She froze in place and felt his hands tighten around hers.

"Love?" he repeated. "Maybe. I've not dug that deep. But Ellie, the carousel is almost complete, and when it is I'll have no choice but to move on."

"No choice? Why? Must you hurry off? Can't you stay on awhile longer?"

"Not if I don't know where we stand. Not if we can't get past this distrust that has you doubting my every move and intent."

"I don't want to distrust you. But nothing happened here before you came. And you've said yourself that it's eerily reminiscent of your time on Coney. Even Sheldon. . ." Her words tapered off. There wasn't a need to bring the other man into the conversation.

A muscle worked in Bascom's jaw. "What about Sheldon?"

"It's nothing." She relaxed her hands in his and watched as his right thumb traced the length of her left one.

He squeezed. "It's something or you wouldn't have brought it up."

A sigh escaped. "I shouldn't say anything. But he's voiced his concern a few times, too, about the similarity of the events matching up to what happened to your wife."

Hurt passed through his eyes again. "And you still believe I had something to do with that?" He shook his head in disgust, and this time he pulled away, taking up the oar and pulling it firmly through the water to spin the boat toward home.

Did she? She didn't answer immediately, wanting to be sure her words were genuine. She said a quick prayer and felt peace descend. "You know what? I don't. Bascom, I trust you in every way. I think I've known it in my heart all along, but sometimes my worries carry more clout than they should."

She reached out and touched his arm, her contact staying his motions. He searched her eyes, and she smiled in return.

"You're sure?"

"I'm sure."

Bascom closed his eyes and let out a sigh of relief. "Thank you."

They sat staring for moments before both leaned forward in unison. Bascom cupped her chin in his hand and tilted it up to meet his kiss. Emotions exploded through Ellie, and a sob caught her throat. He kissed her several more times before they pulled apart, and he gently pushed her hair back from her face.

"Why are you crying? That wasn't my intent."

"Mine, either. But I've been alone so long. I doubt my every move and question my every thought. You bring out emotions in me that are overpowering, but in such a safe way that I feel I can finally let go, that I have someone on my side. But. . ."

She stopped.

"But?" He jiggled her hands, encouraging her to go on.

"But. . .you might leave soon, and I don't know how I'll deal with that."

"Or I might stay. How will you deal with that?" he teased.

She wiped at a tear. "Really?"

"Really. If you'll have me."

"We have that workshop out past the pavilion. Maybe you could set up shop there and stay around awhile? You could still work on other clients' orders."

A smile lit Bascom's face from one side to the other. "You're sure?"

She nodded. "I'd like that."

"On one condition."

"A condition?" She quirked an eyebrow at him. "And what might that be?"

"I've had some ideas about the resort. I'd like to share them with you. Do you trust me? Completely?"

"I do."

"Okay, then. Every night I've heard you tell Prissy your Whimsy tales. They're good. Very good. I think you should write them into booklets and share them with your guests and others who might be interested."

"Oh goodness, no. I couldn't."

"Why not?"

"Well, because. . .they're personal. They're just entertaining little snippets for Priscilla. No one else is going to enjoy them like she does."

"And again I ask, why not?"

"Because. . .they're. . .whimsical. Not many people have time for fluff like that."

"Other children don't deserve a touch of whimsy in their lives?"

"Of course they do, but their parents will provide that, suited to their own child's nature."

Bascom smirked at her. "And you think all parents can just pull stories out of their heads on a whim like you do?"

"Yes. And much better suited to their own child's nature, too. Prissy loves tales of the sea and adventure, but not all children would like that. Some might prefer stories about the animals of the woods or creatures from the desert around their own homes."

"You have no concept of your ability, do you?"

Ellie shook her head to clear it. "Concept of my ability? I'm afraid I don't understand."

"You have no idea the talent it takes to create a story such as yours. You have a gift. You should share it with children and families that don't naturally have the ability to create a make-believe world of their child's dreams."

"Your parents didn't tell you stories at bedtime? Mine did. And my grandparents told stories before that. It's just something we've always done."

Bascom caressed her fingers again, muddling her ability to think. "Maybe so, but you have a knack for it that most other people don't."

"And. . ." He again jiggled her wrist, and she returned her attention from his fascinating hands back to his face.

"And?"

"And I've seen Prissy's drawings as you spin your story. They're quite good."

"They're stick figures and outlines of her imaginings. A child's sketches, nothing more."

"But I'm telling you, they'd sell and sell well. If she draws the most simple of pictures and you write down your tales, we could sell them and bring in more money for the resort."

She smiled at him. "You're serious."

"Very much so. At Coney there were people who made good money just drawing a caricature of the tourists. The rendition suited the person's features, but in a silly, overdone way. Priscilla's drawings are much better than that."

"Hmm. I'll give it some thought. With you and Sheldon around, Wanda and I have been able to turn our attention to other pursuits. Before, we worked nonstop." She glanced up at him and saw his eyes were gentle and completely focused on her words. "I know you didn't come here planning to get so involved in the day-to-day running of the resort, but I hope you know how much we appreciate your help."

"I've enjoyed it, too. I'm glad we could make your life easier, as much as we've also complicated things and brought worry and fear along, too."

Ellie now realized what her heart and head tried to tell her all along—the man sitting before her had nothing to do with the vandalism at the resort or his wife and child's death. She regretted letting the notion fill her mind for even a moment. "I'm so sorry. I know whatever is going on around here is either coincidental or completely out of your hands. I trust you, Bascom. Completely. Please forgive me for ever doubting you."

"You have every right to suspect me."

"No, I don't. You deserve the benefit of doubt just like everyone else. And Bascom. . .I have an idea, too! If you want to help out, why don't you create miniatures of your carousels and let us sell those, too." Ellie almost tipped the boat with her enthusiasm. "We can set up that front corner of the pavilion—the entry—as a small shop of sorts. Maybe we could even open a refreshment stand and offer food items to bring in guests from other resorts."

Bascom steadied the boat and contemplated her words. "Are there enough people in the area?"

"I think so. We all encourage our guests to sample the amenities at each other's places. With Saltair closing down due to the receding water, there's need of another diversion out this way. It might be temporary until they get back on their feet, but for now, we could give it a try."

"You might have something here." Bascom quickly rescued the oar that Ellie's fervor had knocked overboard. "I could do some small carvings. We'll have to discuss it some more. But for now," he motioned to the storm clouds that hung on the far horizon, "we'd best get back to solid ground and batten down the hatches before that next storm hits. Saltair might not have anything to worry about if the rain keeps up."

"Another storm? Goodness. But they're fleeting, so the rain doesn't add up very fast."

The brightness of mood brought on by their clearing the air dimmed as the storm clouds filled the sky. Ellie shivered and knew the sudden urge she had to return to shore had nothing to do with the man sitting across from her.

fourteen

Bascom rowed hard, using both oars to push his way through the rapidly building waves. He'd been so caught up in Ellie and their conversation that he'd missed the approach of the oncoming storm. He'd never forgive himself if he allowed something to happen to Ellie while she remained under his care.

A gust of wind caught up Ellie's hat. Even as she reached for it, the wind pulled it from her head and sent it spinning across the water. It landed a good four yards away and rode flat upon the waves. He faltered, glancing at Ellie for her reaction.

"Let it go. We need to get back to the dock." She had to yell to be heard over the rising wind. Though her words said to move on, her eyes said otherwise, anguish pulling at their depths.

"It's important to you."

She nodded. "It was my last gift from my husband before he passed away. But if he were here, he'd rather us make it safely to shore than worry over a trifle object and risk our lives. Please, continue on to shore."

The last word carried through on a sob in her effort to remain brave and do the right thing. Bascom made a quick decision and turned the boat slightly in the direction of the floating straw contraption. The wind helped them reach it in moments, and he snagged one of the long ties with an oar and pulled it close to the boat. After leaning down to retrieve it, he smiled into Ellie's grateful eyes, but the worry that lay behind the expression urged him to hurry on.

Thunder rumbled overhead and lightning flashed in the distance. The lake wasn't a safe place to be in a storm. Rain began to pelt against them, and Bascom had to squint to see through the deluge that soon surrounded them. Ellie rocked the boat as she cautiously moved to the bench next to him, her presence reassuring.

"Give me an oar. We'll go faster if we both row."

Bascom shook his head and continued to make progress, albeit inches at a time it seemed. He might be tiring, but he wasn't about to let Ellie exert herself because of his poor planning.

"Bascom, give me an oar. Who do you think does my rowing for me when you aren't around? We'll make better time, and we don't have a moment to lose. Now let go of any ridiculous male notions and allow me to help."

She refused to budge, so he lifted the oar up and let her slide underneath before he settled it against her lap. She instantly clutched it and began to push with all her might. He had to admit they immediately made better time as they focused on their own sides.

"We make a good team," he called to her with a grin as they neared the dock. Though she sat inches away, she had to lean close as the wind tried to blow his words away.

"Like two oxen strapped to the same plow, that's us," she laughed back, relief evident as she handed him the oar and crept cautiously forward to the bow.

He used an oar to push closer to shore, and Ellie wrestled the rope and grabbed on to the dock. With practiced skill, she wrapped the braided material around the post and cautiously jumped onto solid ground. He waited to make sure she was stable and then quickly followed suit. He tied his end to the other post, and they hurried up the walkway to shore. Wild waves crashed against the beach, and the wood dock groaned at the onslaught.

"I see Priscilla waiting on the porch—let's head that way." Ellie called over her shoulder, but Bascom would have followed her anywhere, even without the invite.

"Mama, Mama, hurry!" Prissy's worried voice carried to them. "Don't let the thunders get you. C'mon! Run, Mr. Anthony!"

"Prissy, stay put." They'd reached the stairs, and Prissy lunged for her mother, tears coursing down her face. After a moment's hesitation, Ellie pulled the little girl into her embrace. "We're going to have to stop these wet hugs, don't you think?" Priscilla didn't move. Bascom felt exhausted and knew Ellie had to be even more tired. They were both emotionally drained from their talk and physically drained by their adventurous return from the water. "Let me get her."

Though she initially resisted, Prissy finally let him pull her into his arms, and he carried her into the bright warmth of the parlor.

"Oh goodness, let me get you some blankets. Prissy, I told you to wait inside." Wanda looked flustered as she hurried into the room. "I only left her a moment to check the hot cocoa. I thought you'd return soon and knew that a warm drink would be welcome."

"It sounds mighty nice, Wanda, but maybe we'd better get into some dry clothes first."

"Of course. Let me take Prissy and you two can do just that."

"She's soaked through, too." Ellie laughed. "She met us on the porch, but I'm afraid our hug of greeting messed up your plans to keep her dry. "I'll just take her with me, and we'll be back out here shortly."

She reached for her daughter.

Bascom waved her away. "I'll carry her to your door."

Wanda hurried back to the kitchen while the three of them continued on through the back hall.

Prissy laid her head upon Bascom's shoulder and felt like a cuddly rag doll in his arms. He didn't want to release the warm and snuggly girl to her mother. But her dress was damp, and Bascom knew she risked becoming ill with the cold. He could hold her later.

"We'll meet you in the parlor." Ellie reached for Priscilla, her eyes softening as she took in the sight of him holding her daughter with such concern. "Unless Prissy falls asleep. I think her vigil on the porch drained her. As relaxed as she appears to be, once she gets into warm clothes, she might drop off for a nap."

"Not tired, Mama," Priscilla's drowsy voice stated.

They exchanged grins over her head at her denial.

"Warm clothes will feel good," Bascom agreed. He wished he could join the ladies and all three could catch a nap together—as a family. The thought startled him, but he knew their day in the boat had solidified his feelings for Ellie and Priscilla. He wanted to be around to care for both of them, to be their shelter in the storm. He mulled over the protective thought and hurried off to don dry clothes.

❧

Ellie laid her lethargic daughter on their bed and peeled her own drenched clothes off before helping Prissy out of hers. If she tried to change the little girl while as soaked as she was, her daughter would be dripping wet again in no time. Since the back of Prissy's dress had remained dry, she simply pulled a warm quilt over her daughter to keep her warm in the meantime.

She made quick work at changing into a simple pink dress then helped her daughter into a warm nightgown. Since the day promised to remain dreary and with the late afternoon hour, Ellie doubted Prissy would wake before nightfall. And if she did, it wouldn't be a problem for her to take a light dinner in the kitchen in her gown.

Ellie wished she could do the same. Though most of the time she loved running the small resort, there were other times she longed for a private home where she could settle in away from the public and while away her day as she pleased. If nothing else, a small getaway far from all neighbors would be a welcome respite.

She shook off the silly notions and turned her attention to her hair. After the hat had blown off, the wind had taken advantage and whipped the long strands into a fine mess. She pulled the tangled locks from the braid and brushed her hair into shape before winding it up at the nape of her neck. The hair would dry better this way, but again she longed to be able to leave it down and not worry. It wouldn't be appropriate to be so casual in front of her guests, though, and there were Bascom and Sheldon to consider, too.

She felt a warmth flow across her cheeks when her thoughts turned to Bascom. She loved the man. She'd realized it that afternoon as they'd talked in the boat. She sank down onto her dressing table chair and laid her forehead against the cool table. She knew it was time for a heartfelt prayer.

"Oh heavenly Father, would it be possible for Bascom and me to move into the permanent relationship of marriage? I'd love to have a steadfast man like him in my life again." She paused in her musings and wondered at the prayer. Did she really want to move into marriage again? Had she known the man long enough? Not long ago she questioned his very sanity, and now she questioned hers. "I know You led him here, and I know You must have a plan beyond the attraction he's building for our resort, Lord. I feel that You used my grandfather's last request to further that plan. I know You've given me a peace about Bascom's intentions, and that he intends to bring only good to myself and Prissy. He's so gentle with her, and I know he'd never hurt either of us. If You could see fit, I'd love to see an end to the destruction and vandalism and let the guilty party be caught. And then I'd feel free to go ahead and pursue a future with Bascom."

Ellie ended her prayer and raised her head and peeked at her reflection in the mirror. Her eyes sparkled with a newfound joy. Joy in finding her way to God and finding her way back to love. She hopped to her feet and with a last peek at her daughter hurried out the door and into the waiting company of the man she hoped held their future.

She entered the room to find Wanda, Sheldon, and Bascom all there ahead of her. "Sorry I took so long."

"Where's Prissy?" Sheldon looked past Ellie with concern. "I'd hoped to challenge her at a game of checkers."

"She's dead to the world, and I doubt she'll wake before morning. She still needs a nap every few days and hasn't had one for a while. She's played hard today, and I'm sure it's finally catching up with her. I've tucked her in and will check on her in a bit. If she wakes, we'll feed her a little something and send her back on her way."

"She's not been herself all day. I think she's coming down with something." Wanda's forehead creased with concern.

Ellie felt a frown crease her forehead, too, as she thought back to her daughter's countenance. "I didn't notice that she felt warm, but you're right. Now that I think of it, she's quite tired, even more than usual after a long and eventful day."

"And she felt warm in my arms." Bascom stood and offered Ellie his chair. "I thought it was due to our being damp, though, and her coming from inside. Maybe we should go check on her?"

"I think she'll be fine for now, since I just left her."

Sheldon carefully placed his empty mug of cocoa on a doily on the nearby oak table. "Call me if you need me. I want to go out and finish my last piece for the carousel. The unveiling will be tomorrow, correct?"

Bascom grinned Ellie's way, and her stomach tumbled in response. "It is. I can't wait to show it off and see your reaction." Though his words answered Sheldon's question, his eyes were for her only.

Sheldon laughed and excused himself. "I can see that you two would like to be alone. Don't worry, I'll see myself out."

"Nonsense, I'll walk you." Wanda sounded just as anxious to get out of the room and away from the two of them. "Ellie, most of the guests have taken an early dinner and retired to their rooms for the evening. You relax."

Ellie watched as Sheldon held the door to the kitchen open for her friend. A moment later, she heard the far kitchen door open and close from the hallway, and then the door swung partly open as the outer door let Sheldon into the brunt of the storm.

"He should have waited for things to let up. Now he'll be as drenched as we were."

"I don't think he minds. He likes to be alone to tie up his loose ends. I'm sure he figures I'll be busy for a while and he can putter to his heart's content. The carousel is all but finished, but he's a perfectionist and likes to go over every inch to make sure everything's ready for the big day."

Ellie eyed the storm outside the window. "If it continues like this. . .I'm not sure there will be an unveiling tomorrow. We'll be lucky if even the guests try to venture out in this."

A huge crash from the back of the house had Ellie jumping to her feet. "Prissy!"

She hurried through the back hallway and met up with a frazzled Wanda.

"It's just the door—it blew open. Sheldon must not have latched it completely."

The back door swung freely on its hinges, the wind slamming it against the wall as rain poured into the space around them. Bascom hurried to close it, a battle of wills that he finally won. He returned to Ellie's side.

"I'll go check on Priscilla," Ellie said. "I need to make sure the noise didn't wake her and scare her." She hastened into their room. The only light came from the almost constant streaks of lightning that continued to illuminate the world outside their window. But the erratic flashes were enough to show Ellie everything she needed to see.

Prissy's side of the bed lay empty.

fifteen

Ellie reentered the hall. "Wanda, could Prissy have snuck into the kitchen without your knowing?" Her voice shaky, she knew the question sounded incoherent even as she asked it. "Maybe the storm scared her and she hid under the table or something?"

"No, I'm sure I would have heard her come in. She's not in the room?"

"No. I left her in bed sound asleep. There isn't any way she'd wake up on her own. Not as tired as she was." She noticed muddy footprints on the wood floor near the door. Her voice rose and panic set in as she pointed them out to the others. "What if someone's taken her?"

"She has to be close by." Wanda's voice dropped to a choked whisper. "We need to check under the bed and behind furniture."

"I checked the entire room. There aren't many hiding places."

"Let's be realistic. If the crash startled her, would she have been able to hide this fast? We got here within moments, and Ellie, you went right in to check on her." Bascom's comments were the first to make sense.

Wanda, clearly flustered, put a shaking hand to her forehead. "Then I'll go upstairs and you all search down here. She wouldn't have gone far."

Bascom sent Ellie a concerned look. "She couldn't have gotten past us. The back door is the only obvious choice. You'd have heard her enter the kitchen, and we'd have seen her enter the parlor. Your grandmother's in her room resting, right? And these wet footprints. . .someone had to have come in from outside."

Ellie's knees gave way, and she almost sank to the floor. She fought the sensation, though, and stayed on her feet. "Then you agree—someone has taken my daughter."

Bascom dropped down to inspect the footprints from a closer angle. He held a lantern above them.

"Tell me what you're thinking, Bascom." Ellie placed her hand on his shoulder, both as a way to feel his solid strength and to capture his attention.

"You don't think she'd go out on her own? Maybe to find us if she didn't completely wake up and thought maybe you were out there since the door stood open?"

"No." Though Ellie tried to sound strong, she failed miserably. "She's a heavy sleeper. She wouldn't have been able to wake that fast and get up. She'd have been sitting up in bed, waiting for me to come."

"What about your grandmother's room?"

"You said yourself she wouldn't have had time to get there after the crash."

She hurried through their personal parlor and looked into her grandmother's room. Prissy wasn't there. She rejoined the others.

"Then where else could she be?" Bascom paced the short hall. "You're absolutely sure she wouldn't have ventured outdoors if she did wake up confused?"

"I don't know. But I doubt it. Storms scare her." The thought of her daughter out there, possibly alone, sent tremors of horror through Ellie's body. The thought of her out there, not alone, brought along worse thoughts. "Bascom, if she did go, she'll never make it out there. You can't see two feet in front of your face, and she'll be lost in moments. The lake is too close and violent. If she falls in. . ." She stared up at him. "And what if someone has her? Those footprints didn't appear on their own."

Her legs no longer held her up, and she sank to the floor. "Oh, Prissy!"

Wanda's voice carried over to them from where she prayed for Prissy's safety.

Bascom took Ellie by the arms. "Ellie, we're going to find her. We need to pull together. We don't have a moment to lose. We've lost enough time as it is. I'm going for Sheldon, and you go round up the guests. Look everywhere you can think of where she might have hidden in the house. Do you understand?"

Ellie forced herself to nod. She had to get a grip. Her daughter needed her.

Bascom hurried into the storm, shutting the door behind him.

Though Bascom seemed inclined to point the finger of suspicion away from foul play, Ellie knew in her heart her daughter hadn't snuck off on her own to hide in fear. She ignored Bascom's directions and, instead, went into Wanda's former room where she pulled Bascom's small gun from a high shelf. She checked to make sure it was loaded and ready and then pulled on an overcoat, determined to join the search outside. Wanda would cover the search inside.

Ellie didn't take time to grab a lantern; the wind would surely blow it right out. Instead, she'd have to count on the lightning for visibility, if such a thing were possible in such blinding rain. She opened the back door, and the wind immediately snatched it from her hold, slamming the heavy wood barrier back into the wall. The strong wind whipped against her as she exited the house, almost knocking her from her feet. She grabbed hold of the banister and got her bearings. She again headed for the outbuilding where they did the laundry. Prissy still liked to play in there and for some strange reason, the room gave her a sense of security.

She pulled her cloak close against her neck with one hand and clutched the gun in the other. She'd never shot anyone before, but if someone had her daughter and meant harm to the little girl, she'd not hesitate to do whatever was needed.

A crash of thunder made her jump, the sound so near she knew the storm now sat directly overhead. She'd almost reached the protection of the washhouse when a strong hand clamped onto her shoulder.

❧

Bascom sighed with relief when Ellie spun around to face him. His relief fled when he noticed the weapon aimed at his heart. He snatched the gun from her shaky grip and ushered her inside the dry room.

"What on earth are you thinking, coming out here armed in this mess? I thought I told you to search the house!"

"There are plenty of people searching in there right now. My abilities are better used out here. We need to find whoever took her and stop him."

"And how do you plan to do that? By shooting some innocent person? How would that help?"

"I didn't shoot you. You snuck up on me from behind and swung me around. I was ready to shoot whoever meant me—or my daughter—harm. If I'd meant to shoot you, you'd be lying on the ground, dead. Now move away and let me continue on. Both of us know Prissy didn't come out here of her own accord, and we both know that someone has taken her. I'll not be wasting my time inside when I can be out here, helping to cover more area." Her hands briefly clutched his jacket front and then slid down his lapel in despair. "Bascom. We're too late. She's probably long gone."

"Don't give up on me, Ellie. I'm going to find your daughter. But I want you to pull yourself together and wait inside the house. Running wild with a gun isn't going to fix matters."

"Standing here arguing won't fix matters, either. You keep the gun, but I'm going to continue my search. I'll go crazy if I have to sit inside, wasting my time while waiting for someone else to find her." She glanced behind him. "You said you were going for Sheldon. . . . Where is he?"

"He wasn't in the pavilion, so I'm searching without him." Bascom softened his voice. "Your time inside won't be a waste if you use it to pray for Priscilla's safety. Trust God, Ellie. I know He'll lead us to her."

"I can pray just fine from where I am."

"Fine. Continue your search, but please use caution." Bascom really wanted to tie her up and carry her back to the house. . .a situation that would surely carry repercussions in their future. But if he couldn't keep her stubborn self safe by force, he could do so with her by his side. It added another dimension to his search, but at least he'd know Ellie was all right. "As a matter of fact, just trail me. I can keep track of you that way."

He didn't miss Ellie's glare or the roll of her eyes, but he was thankful as she fell into step behind him. They exited the small room and reentered the deluge, which immediately engulfed them.

"Stick close to my heels," he yelled. "Grab on to my cloak if you must. But do *not* fall behind."

❧

Ellie heard his command, but the outline of a shadowy figure heading toward the pavilion momentarily distracted her. She knew it could be someone from inside the resort helping with the search, but if so, what was in the bundle the person carried?

She turned to capture Bascom's attention, but he'd already disappeared into the darkness ahead. Without giving further thought to her actions, she turned the opposite way and crept back to the pavilion.

The mud slowed her steps, causing her to slip and slide, but she pushed forward and with the wind at the other end of the building, slipped quietly through the back door and into the room. A flash of lightning lit up the room, and to Ellie's surprise illuminated Sheldon, who knelt in front of Priscilla with his hand clasped over Prissy's tiny mouth.

"Sheldon! You found her!" She started forward and then stopped, confused, as she registered the scene before her.

Bits and pieces of Sheldon's previous conversations flew through Ellie's mind. During the past few weeks, he'd purposely planted doubt about Bascom's past and present actions in order to throw suspicion off himself. All this time she'd suspected the wrong man. And Bascom's trust in his protégé had prevented him from seeing the truth, that the man he trusted the most was the one who least deserved his faith.

Fury roiled through her, and she threw caution to the wind. "Unhand my daughter at once, and move away from her."

She realized her mistake immediately. Sheldon snatched Prissy into his arms and without her weapon, Ellie had no way to bargain for her daughter's safety.

"Mama! Come get me."

Ellie watched as Prissy fought Sheldon's embrace, but the tiny girl's struggling had no effect on his strong grip.

"Sheldon, you're scaring her. Please, let her go and take me instead."

"Why should I do that when at the moment I have you both? You aren't going to leave here without your precious Prissy, now are you?"

Ellie wished for the gun. "No, I'll not leave my daughter.

I'm staying with you, Prissy."

Prissy's sobs filled the air, and she again wrestled against his hold. "Let me go! I want my mama."

"No, it looks like I get more than I bargained for tonight. At first it seemed Bascom would keep you safely contained and out of my reach, but luck is on my side. This will be as much fun as the time I took away his wife and son."

Ellie gasped. "What a horrible thing to say." But he was right. If she'd listened to Bascom, Ellie would be safely inside and perhaps Bascom could have saved Prissy from the crazy man before he brought her to harm. As it was, Bascom now stood to lose them both, which would make him crazy with the pain and guilt.

"Your plan wouldn't have worked. Prissy disappeared while Bascom was with me. I wouldn't have suspected him. You've now convinced me, even though I'd already come to this conclusion, that Bascom is innocent of all you've pointed your finger at."

"Really, does any of that matter now? When you two reach your demise, Bascom will be the sole suspect, and I can move on and continue our trade without him. I know all he had to teach me and have no further need of his instruction."

"But why? As you just said, he trained you. He trusted you with his most valuable possession, his knowledge of creating one-of-a-kind carousels."

"Which is why I have no need of him any longer."

"I know he's taught you of other more important things, just as he has taught me. Such as how to have a relationship with Christ. Bascom's the type of man to hand over the reins of the business to you if it meant you'd leave those he cares about alone."

"I have no desire to learn about his God. And he wouldn't share the possession I most desired—his wife."

"His wife?"

"I had her first. We courted, and she knew my greatest desire would be to train with Bascom. She said she had a way to convince him to take me on as his apprentice. I didn't have any way to know that she enticed him to court her and in the process fell in love with him instead."

"But surely, if he'd known, he'd have ended the relationship out of preference to you?"

"No, by the time I found out, the apprenticeship was well on its way. My *fiancée* made it clear that if I told Bascom anything of our prior relationship, she'd make sure to ruin my future as a carousel designer before it even started."

Ellie felt sick to her stomach. "Bascom had no idea that you'd courted her. Nor did he know of his wife's true nature."

"I suppose he didn't. But that's beside the point. The point is, he ruined my life, and I had to get even. I righted the wrong caused by his wife, and now I'll get even with him by taking over the business he so treasures."

"But if he didn't know you'd courted her first, why would you lash out at him?"

He turned to her with a look that could only be described as pure evil. "Because it makes me feel better."

Ellie froze as Sheldon, thoroughly agitated and working himself into a frenzy, began to pace back and forth in front of the far window. Prissy's terrified cries were muffled by his beefy hand. Ellie wrung her hands, desperate for a way out of the mess. She sent up a prayer for help but knew no one had likely ventured out in the storm, and Bascom had gone on the other way. If she were to free Prissy from this demented man, she'd have to figure out a way to do it herself.

sixteen

The storm continued outside, pounding the roof of the pavilion with a vengeance. Gusts of rain lashed against the windows. Prissy's cries became louder as her terror grew over both the storm and the man who held her hostage.

"Sheldon, let her come to me." Ellie struggled to keep her voice steady, though fury and frustration flowed through her. "At least let her feel the safety of my arms."

Rain pounded against the building, and a loud crash against the north wall caused them all to jump. Prissy wailed, lunging for Ellie. Sheldon had to struggle to keep his hold. He jerked her hard against him and hissed into her ear. "Don't move again."

Ellie struggled to hear Sheldon's words over the brunt of the raging tempest. His mood seemed to match the maelstrom outside the window.

Lord, if ever I've needed You, it's now. Please help me find a way to help my daughter and get her safely away from this madman.

Even as she said the words, she felt clarity flow through her. She needed to stay focused. She'd be lucky to have even one opportunity to free her daughter, and if and when it came, she needed to be ready to make her move.

She glanced up, and lightning illuminated a face in the window. Holding back her scream, she hoped whoever was out there had seen enough to go for help.

❧

Bascom bit back the curse that threatened to explode from his mouth. Instead, he ranted at God. He'd lost a wife and son. Was history destined to repeat itself by taking Ellie and Priscilla from him, too? He'd lived a good life, had continued forward after his huge losses, and for what? Only to again lose the woman and child he loved?

Had Ellie decided to sneak away of her own accord? Or had the same person that snatched Prissy somehow taken her from under his nose, too?

He'd returned to the washhouse, but Ellie wasn't there. He continued the opposite way he'd come. He knew she hadn't passed him while going the other way. For whatever reason, she'd left his protection and turned a different direction.

The wind howled and his hat blew from his head. Ignoring it, he pressed forward. He heard the faint sound of a woman's voice from up ahead. Hoping against hope that the voice belonged to Ellie, he moved forward at a quicker pace. His foot slid out from under him and raw pain shot through his injured ankle as he dropped to his knees. Gasping, he breathed deeply, trying to quell the biting pain. He struggled back to his feet and continued on, ignoring the stab of agony each step brought.

"Bascom." The voice was closer now, but he realized it belonged to Wanda, not Ellie. Disappointment filled him, but he knew they had a better chance as a team.

"Over here." His voice sounded loud and ravaged. He didn't know whether pain or worry caused the infliction. "Stay near the building. Follow the wall."

He did the same, bracing himself against it for support, and within moments Wanda appeared in front of him. She looked as tormented as he felt. The wind had whipped her hair from its usual neat bun, and now the strands stuck to her face where the wind and rain pelted it. Her eyes were wild as she half ran, half crawled to him.

"I heard you yell." She stopped to catch her breath and grabbed his arm. Whether for support or to hold him in place he didn't know. "I found them. Both Priscilla and Ellie. They're in the pavilion. I saw through the window. It's dark, but the lightning flashed, and Sheldon stood just on the other side of the glass. Bascom, he looks demented and has Prissy clutched in his arms."

Bascom momentarily froze in place. "Sheldon? But why. . . He's the one?" He felt as if a vise clamped around his heart. He thought back to their recent conversation. Sheldon had played him for a fool. His voice came out in a tortured whisper. "I trusted him."

"I don't know why, Bascom. I'm so sorry." Wanda touched his arm. "What should we do?"

Bascom hurried forward, and Wanda blocked his path.

"Wanda, if Sheldon has them, even if he has only Prissy, and he's in the pavilion, he must plan to recreate my wife and son's deaths. He'd have to know he couldn't get away with this. I have to get to them."

Bascom shoved past her and moved toward the pavilion. He felt Wanda's hand as she grasped for his sleeve. He shook her off and continued on, his steps slowed by the throbbing ankle.

"Stop." Her voice commanded him to listen, and for a brief moment he did.

"I can't wait for you. Go for help. I need to get Priscilla away from him."

"You won't do any good if you go off half-cocked. It'll take both of us to stop him. I also saw Ellie standing a few feet away from them. The look on her face. . ." She shook her head. "I'll never get it out of my head. She's terrified, Bascom."

Bascom let her words sink in. "All the more reason for me to get in there."

"So you can be at his mercy, too? No. I won't allow it. I came for your help. Not so you could brush me aside and plow over me."

"I'm sorry for that. But now isn't the time for formalities. I have to get to them. Sheldon's been the one all along. And I trusted him. Don't you understand? All my grief, he must have savored it. But why? He's been my apprentice, my best friend. Or so I thought. Yet he killed my wife and son. Wanda, I can't let him do the same to Ellie and Priscilla."

"We don't know if he's armed. We aren't. We need a plan."

Bascom fingered the gun that still rested in his pocket, but didn't say anything to Wanda. She might not be armed, but he was. And in light of things, he couldn't wait to use the weapon against the murderous traitor that awaited him inside.

He thought a minute and then nodded. "I'll take a look first, and then we'll talk about strategy."

They crept closer to the windows, and Wanda motioned to the spot where she'd been standing. Bascom ducked and hesitantly moved forward, suddenly thankful for the storm that hid his approach. Lightning burst around him, and he rose up to peek into the dim interior. As Wanda had said, Sheldon still held Prissy, but now, free of terror, she hung limply in his arms. Ellie was nowhere in sight.

❧

Ellie, livid, had watched in horror when Prissy collapsed in Sheldon's arms. She thrust herself forward, only to have Sheldon block her with a solid arm, honed from years of handling heavy wood, and knock her to the floor with a thud.

"She's fine. She fainted."

"My daughter doesn't faint. You held your hand too tightly against her mouth. You've suffocated her." Her hate-filled words, sharp with venom, lashed out at the man. "You've killed my daughter!"

She couldn't breathe. The thought of losing her daughter brought Ellie such pain that she couldn't remember how to take in air. She clutched at her stomach and rocked back and forth, struggling to catch her breath. "My baby. . ."

Sheldon laughed. "I love the theatrics, Ellie. If you weren't about to meet your end, you'd do well to take up acting." He continued his hold on Priscilla, but resumed his pacing across the room. "And while we're on that topic, did you also act when spending time with me? Was your devotion real? Or was it also contrived?"

"Any devotion toward you on my part had to be imagined. . . but only by your insane mind." Ellie spat the words his way, but he didn't seem to notice the malice. Prissy made a slight mewling sound, and Ellie almost collapsed on the spot with relief. At least he hadn't lied about her daughter's well-being. "Besides, I thought you had intentions toward Wanda."

"Wanda? Not a chance. I only spent time with her out of boredom while waiting for my time with you. But as usual, Bascom had to slide in with his debonair ways and snatch you out from under me."

Ellie couldn't believe this conversation. The man was mad and then some. "There was no 'snatching' or anything else. I've been too busy to think about anything other than the resort. And even if I were looking for a relationship, it wouldn't have been with you. You were nice to talk to—or so I thought—but only in the way of a friend. Now I have to wonder if my very soul somehow sensed your evil."

Sheldon's face crinkled into something wicked. "You did care. I saw it in your eyes and the way you smiled at me. I saw you pull back your window curtain at night, searching the dark for my presence."

"I searched the dark for the madman that terrorized the resort. Unfortunately, my naiveté left you out of that equation. If it hadn't, maybe we'd have known sooner and avoided this unpleasant situation."

"Unpleasant indeed. You're going to meet your Maker tonight. Lucky for you that Bascom has spent so much time talking of the Greater Being that would 'save' you. I guess soon you'll find out whether his story is truth or fiction."

Ellie wasn't getting anywhere with her hatred, so she changed tactics. "Sheldon, I believe in God and everything that Bascom has told me. If you'd take a moment, maybe you'd find out the truth, too. It's not too late."

"No, maybe not, but it will be soon if I don't get on with my plan to dupe Bascom. Then I can stand at his side and watch him grieve for another two years." He grabbed her hair and pulled her to her feet. His voice oozed sarcasm. "Move toward my room over there. I think that's the best place to follow through on my intentions. You can thank your God that Prissy won't be conscious or know what's going on."

Just as they reached the carousel, the outer door blew open. It slammed into the wall with such force that Sheldon lost his grip on Prissy. Taking advantage of his distracted state, Ellie threw her body against his and clutched at her daughter. Another body came from the other direction, and Ellie held on to Prissy and protected her as they fell to the floor. Lantern light filled the room, and Ellie glanced up to see Wanda near the back door, dripping wet, while holding the lantern from Sheldon's room high in the air.

❧

Ellie pulled Prissy close and scuttled back toward the wall as Bascom pounded the cowering form of Sheldon. Rain poured into the room until Wanda set the lantern on the carousel's base and hurried over to fight the door closed. The sudden change in loudness roused Prissy.

"It's okay, baby. It's okay. Mama has you now."

Prissy cried softly and clung to Ellie. Wanda hurried over to gather them both in her arms. They sat as a group of three and watched as Bascom towered over Sheldon's prostrate body, lifted a small revolver, and pressed it firmly against Sheldon's head. He cocked the gun.

"Bascom, no!" Ellie hurried to hand Prissy to Wanda and crawled to Bascom's side. "Stop. You don't want to do this."

"Oh, but I do. You'll never know how much I'm savoring the fact that I get to personally put an end to all the pain Sheldon has caused. I get to watch his eyes as I pull the trigger. I want to feel the power of justice done. I want to see him as he goes to his demise."

"It isn't your place, Bascom." She reached over and tilted the top of the gun away from Sheldon's head. Bascom froze in place and glowered at her. "You'll get your justice as you watch the sheriff take him away. And at his trial. If you end things now, it will be over for him. Let the law take control, Bascom, and let Sheldon suffer the consequences legally. Will that not be more justice? To let him sit and rot in a jail cell as he contemplates his fate?"

Still Bascom didn't move.

She dropped her voice to a whisper. "Do you forever want Prissy's mind to carry the image of what she's about to witness at your hands?"

This time her words hit their mark and a look of devastation crossed his features. He remained as he was, with a knee pressed against Sheldon's back, but the hand holding the gun dropped limply to his lap. "What has become of me? What am I thinking?"

"You're thinking a lot of unanswered questions have suddenly been answered, and the answer you were looking for is here along with a lot of pain. It's going to be all right, Bascom."

He reached up and pulled her into his arms, careful to keep the loaded weapon pointed away from her. She leaned into his embrace.

"I'll go for help. You keep him covered." She stood and hurried over to Wanda.

Prissy propelled herself into Ellie's waiting arms.

Wanda waved her toward the door. "You go ahead. I'll stay here with them."

They both froze as they heard another click of the gun.

seventeen

"I'm sorry I startled you yesterday when I reset the trigger." Bascom scrunched his face into a grimace.

The bright early morning sun shone down upon them as they strolled along the shoreline of the lake, their hands tentatively interlaced. It seemed forever ago that Ellie had felt the security of having her hand held in a man's strong grip. Her thoughts couldn't be farther away from the previous night's events. It took her a moment to catch up with his thoughts, but when she did, she sent him a playful look. "Don't worry about it. The scare kept my mind off the raging storm that I had to carry Prissy through."

He tugged at her, pulling her closer against his side, and she laughed. They walked in silence for a few moments, enjoying the serenity of the lakeside after the furious storm of the previous day. Though the sky showed no trace of the gray clouds, the ground gave testament that they'd suffered mightily from the wind. Debris lined the water's edge, and pieces of wood and cloth bobbed on the water's surface.

Ellie shuddered at what might have been. "Prissy could have wandered into this mess."

"No, Sheldon admitted he snuck back in and took her straight from her bed to the pavilion. He only hesitated to see if the storm would die out, but when he heard you yelling, he hurried on into the brunt of it, which must have been when you saw him."

"And now? What happened after I left the pavilion?"

Bascom chuckled. "You mean after you sent the retired sheriff to aid me? His wife said he was happier than she'd seen him in years when you came through that door, first because you had Priscilla safely in your arms, but then because you sent him to my side. I guess he's been at loose ends of late and relished the occasion to step back into the role of defender of the law."

"So, did he send one of the other men for the sheriff in town?"

"No. He insisted no one go out into the storm and instead sat with Sheldon all night, keeping him under armed guard until I could ride out at daybreak to bring back the law."

"I'm glad someone benefitted from this awful mess. I still don't understand why Sheldon did it all. He explained his reasoning to me, but it doesn't make any sense. Why didn't he have it out with you from the start? If your wife truly loved him, then she moved on, why didn't he just accept that and do the same?"

Bascom sighed. "I'm not sure we'll ever understand the whys and where-to-fors of Sheldon's mind."

Ellie worried her lower lip and contemplated his answer that wasn't really an answer.

"Do you think it's true your wife loved him first?" Immediately she realized the inappropriateness of her question and retracted her comment. "I'm sorry. That was beyond insensitive. This all has to be so painful for you. Don't bother formulating an answer to such a heartless question."

"No. It's a fair question." Bascom looked at her, his pain-filled eyes tugging at her heart. "I've thought about it all night, and I've not come up with an answer. My wife did insist that Sheldon be a part of everything we did. She's the one that begged me to train him under the pretense that it would allow me more time for her. But looking back, she resented carrying my son. I thought she'd adjust after his birth, but instead she seemed to grow more distant and angry. She compared Sheldon's carefree life to our life many times. Maybe she wished she had married him instead. I don't know. But justice has finally been served. Sheldon was caught. And nothing will bring my son back. Trying to figure everything out, well, we'll probably never know answers to all of it."

"I really am sorry, Bascom. I know it has to hurt to think your wife wasn't as faithful as you thought."

Bascom stopped, turned her to face him, and grasped her other hand. "There were lots of things, signs, that if I'd stopped to pay more attention, would have shown me the truth earlier. I'm sure of it now that I look back. Instead I buried myself in work and hoped things would settle down with time."

"But they didn't."

"No. Instead I lost everything. . .but in the process I gained my relationship with God and came through the pain a stronger person. Nothing will ever replace the loss of my son, but I know he's in a better place now and one day I'll be reunited with him."

"And your wife?" Ellie forced herself to breathe. She hated asking him these questions, but they slipped out of their own accord. And deep down she knew she had to hear where he stood on each topic.

"My wife, to my knowledge, never stepped foot in a church or read the Word of God. The few times I tried to get her to go for our son's sake, she laughed in my face. So as I said, I worked. We didn't go to church."

"If it wasn't for you, Bascom, I'd be in the same place. Thank you for caring enough to share the love of the Lord with me."

"You're more than welcome. I'm glad good came from my presence after all the mess I brought along. Maybe it's wrong, but I feel a measure of relief now that the mystery of both places is solved. I'm just sorry we didn't catch on quicker. He threw us off with the vandalism to the other resorts. I wish things had been different, but the facts are what they are. I'll have to work through things, and I know I'll have a lot of things to talk out with God over the next few months, but for the first time in a long time, I feel I can move forward with my life." Complete peace shone through Bascom's eyes for the first time since they met up on the front porch earlier in the day—when he'd grabbed her in a strong, protective hug. After he'd assured himself that she was safe and all was well, the peaceful expression had quickly changed to one of remorse.

Bascom now smiled at her with that familiar crooked grin and pulled her close, his eyes searching hers with a glow of discovery, as if he'd just found a treasure. Her heart picked up its pace as he leaned down and gently brushed his lips across hers.

"Am I a part of that future?" Her voice sounded breathless even to her own ears.

"I sure hope so, Ellie. You and Priscilla both. This is all new to me, but I didn't sleep much last night, and I did give the future some thought. What I'd like would be to stick around and help you here at the resort while basing my creations out of the area." His thumb caressed hers, momentarily distracting her as it sent little trills up her hand and arm. She forced herself to focus.

"You'd still travel and do your carousels, then." She couldn't explain her disappointment, though she knew in part it had to do with the fact that she needed to stay to run the place and couldn't afford to shut down and travel if they were to marry.

A flush warmed her face as she realized how far her own thoughts had strayed, all because of a silly kiss. He hadn't even mentioned marriage. Maybe he had friendship in mind, a protective alliance of sorts. She needed a man around, and he needed a place to live. But deep down she knew it was more than that. A realization hit and a smile formed on her lips. The kiss a few moments earlier had nothing to do with friendship. And it had everything to do with romance. It had enough passion behind it that maybe her thoughts of marriage weren't too far from the mark. The warmth of the flush returned.

Bascom chuckled. "I'm not sure where your thoughts have gone, but I hope the expression on your face bodes well for our relationship. To answer your question, I'd like to stay put and ship the carousels anywhere they need to go. I can interview the purchaser on paper and still custom design each creation. I have some other ideas I'll tell you about later, other ways to make a living with my wood carving. And if I were to take on a carousel project and if I were to travel, if we were married. . . you and Prissy could tag along as a holiday for the short time we'd need to be away. I'm sure we could arrange for someone to watch over things here while we were gone."

Tears filled Ellie's eyes. "Is that a proposal?"

Bascom laughed. "Not the best one I could offer, but yes, it's a very clumsy attempt at one." His words were light, but his eyes were serious as he waited for her answer.

Speechless for once, Ellie only nodded.

He grabbed her up and swung her around in a circle.

Her delighted laugh at his unexpected jubilance rang out. "Oh my. What would people think if they saw us?"

"They'd know they were observing a very special moment." A beautiful smile transformed his features. Bascom closed his eyes and shook his head as if to clear it. "Let me try this again so I can do it properly." His blue eyes softened as he met her gaze. "Ellie, will you marry me? You can take all the time you need, but I know in my heart it's what I want."

"It's what I want, too, and I don't need a lot of time."

"I promise I'll do everything in my power to make you and Prissy happy."

"You've already made us happy, Bascom. I can't imagine a better ending to the past week's events than this."

"How about we forget all that and look at it as our new beginning?"

"That sounds wonderful. So. . .shall we go share the news?"

"I'd be delighted."

Now, with their hands clutched tighter than before, they began their walk back toward the resort.

"I have a question." Ellie glanced sideways at him.

"Just one?" His eyes twinkled in humor at what must surely seem to be her hundredth question of the morning. "Is it the last?"

"Probably not." She looked toward him, squinted into the sun, and sent him a smirk. "How did you know where to find us last night? You arrived just in the nick of time."

"Ah, the question I've been waiting to hear. Wanda saw you and came for me."

"She was the face in the window!"

"Apparently so. And as we crept around the building, trying to figure out a plan, a barrel rammed into the wall, barely missing her leg. We hurried along, but after seeing the distraction the loud bang caused Sheldon, we knew he was jumpy and came up with a plan."

"And the plan was. . . ," Ellie urged him on when he paused, the playful twinkle still in his eyes. "Don't keep me waiting."

"The plan was, she'd throw open the door and cause a diversion to block any noise I might make while sneaking through the back."

"Apparently it worked."

"Indeed it did. And Ellie. . ."

Ellie snuggled against him as his arm wrapped around her shoulders. "Yes?"

"I promise to do everything in my ability to never make you wait. That promise includes any further wait when it comes to the carousel. The unveiling will still be tonight."

eighteen

"Mama, Mama, hurry up! Everybody's waiting." Prissy's dramatic voice carried down the hallway and through the open door just before she danced through the opening.

"Everybody?" Ellie teased. Though they'd invited all their guests and a few neighbors to visit the carousel for its unveiling, Ellie would first receive a private showing so she could savor the moment without anyone else present.

"Grammy is serving refreshments on the front porch. I got an extra specially big sugar cookie and a glass of lemonade, too."

Which accounted for her daughter's intensified exuberance at the moment. If the excitement of the event and unveiling wasn't enough to make her daughter bounce off the walls, sweets always made Prissy extra bouncy.

"Can I go get another cookie while I wait?"

"No! I mean, no, I'm almost ready. Let me take one more quick peek in the mirror, and we'll head out."

"Mr. Bascom Anthony is waiting for us out back."

Hop, hop, hop. She tripped on her blue calico skirt and catapulted into Ellie's side. Ellie stayed her with her hands.

"Settle down, honey. And you know you don't have to call him by all his names. Mr. Bascom or Mr. Anthony is just fine for now."

"But I like to call him by all his names. No one else does, so it's special. Until I can call him by his really special name. Daddy. After we get married, I get to call him that, right?"

Ellie quirked the side of her mouth up and smiled in amusement. "Right."

"Are you ready *now*?" Prissy formed her mouth into a pout.

" 'Cause we've waited a very long time for you to see your surprise. I don't even get a ride until you see it. We both get to go on the...the...maiden foyage."

"Maiden voyage?"

"Yep. Maiden foyage." She hopped toward the door. "C'mon, let's *go!*"

"I'm ready, daughter." Ellie settled her hat at a jaunty angle on her head. The hat matched her mood. She reached for Prissy's hand.

"Mr. Bascom Anthony! We're coming!" Prissy bellowed down the hall.

Ellie heard his rich laugh from the back porch. He stepped into sight just outside the door. He made a show of checking his watch before tucking it slowly into his trouser pocket.

"It's about time." He sent her his crooked grin.

Ellie's heart fluttered. Even without the newfound sparkle in his brilliant blue eyes, the man was extremely handsome. The soft breeze tugged at his hair, which again looked ready for a visit with Gram's shears. But she rather liked it this way.

"I'm right on time and you know it," she teased back. "The both of you would do well to learn some patience."

"Patience? We've waited how long now to show you this creation?" Bascom played along.

"Forever!" Prissy joined in.

They began to walk toward the pavilion.

Ellie strolled leisurely between the two of them. "Hardly forever. You haven't known about the carousel forever, Priscilla."

She turned to Bascom. "And you. You might have had the structure in mind a bit longer than Priscilla, but you only finished it yesterday."

Bascom rubbed his chin in contemplation. "Are you sure? It seems it's been much longer." He sent a questioning look to Prissy.

Prissy giggled and nodded. "It has only been a day. But

we've been building it for much longer. And we need our maiden foyage."

"Prissy!" Now Bascom clutched at his heart, feigning indignation. "Are you giving away our secrets?" He reached over and tucked Ellie's arm around his other one.

"No, not secrets, only hints."

"So, maiden voyage is a hint, hmm? I thought you were planning a carousel, not a ship." Ellie reached over to tug one of Prissy's dark braids.

"Mama, it's beautiful. Just you wait and see." Prissy's voice became breathless as they neared the building. "Can I run ahead?"

"Sure." Bascom's voice held a hint of mischief. "Wait for us just inside. Tell Wanda we're ready."

Prissy squealed and hurried off.

Ellie looked at him, eyebrows raised.

"What?" He shrugged. "Is it wrong for a man to want a moment alone with his future bride?"

A shiver ran up Ellie's arm as he caressed her hand that hugged his arm. She laid her head against his shoulder, and they walked in companionable silence. As they neared the door, his footsteps slowed. Ellie could hear the sound of an organ from inside the building in front of them.

Ellie looked up at him. "What is it?"

He scowled, looked toward the entrance, and then back at her. "I've never felt this nervous about an unveiling before. I know you'll like it, yet. . ."

"Yet what? How could I not love something you've made with your own artistic hands? I'd love it even if it had nothing to do with me."

"I just want you to be happy."

"I am happy." Ellie could feel the glow reflecting from her face. How could he not see it as well?

He apparently did because relief replaced the scowl, and he

grinned her way. "So you're ready?"

"More than. Let me see your creation!"

Prissy stood in the doorway, giggling. She waved inside, and the music grew louder. A wispy piece of fabric hung over the doorway, and Bascom pushed it aside so they could enter the building.

They stopped just inside and waited for Ellie's eyes to adjust to the dim interior. Soft gas lighting lit the room, adding a dreamy quality to the fantasy scene before them. The transformation that had taken place in the room took Ellie's breath away, but her eyes were drawn immediately to the centerpiece, the magnificent carousel in the middle of the room.

THE LAND OF WHIMSY had been hand lettered in elegant script around the side of the carousel's canopy. Wooden seashells and starfish, painted in bright colors to match the sea creatures, framed the words and disappeared out of sight around the curve of the roof. The entire structure seemed to embody the many characters from her stories.

"You've captured Whimsy." Her voice was an awestruck whisper. "It's beautiful."

Bascom and Prissy each took hold of one of Ellie's hands and led her to the platform. She stepped onto the wooden floor of the structure, which wobbled slightly under her weight. Priscilla hopped up beside her, Bascom at her heels. The late afternoon sunlight beamed through the many windows and reflected off the shiny creatures that stood side by side in sets of two around the circumference of the platform. Seahorses, dolphins, huge fish, and even stingrays painted with vivid color and wearing expressions of pure joy danced around before her.

A laugh bubbled out from her. "I absolutely love it!"

She walked around the circle, trailing her hands softly across each carved piece.

"Look, Mama! Jewels. Just like pirate treasure." Prissy pointed out the various jewels that sparkled brilliantly in the sunlight.

Ellie watched as her daughter rubbed her finger over a large sapphire blue gem that had been inset into a dolphin's saddle.

"Are you ready for a ride?" Ellie, so lost in her musings, jumped as Bascom leaned close to her ear.

"It's time for our maiden foyage?" Prissy's voice rose several octaves.

"Aye, 'tis finally time, Princess Priscilla." Bascom swung her up into his arms. "Would you prefer your maiden voyage to be upon the Mighty Schooner?"

Perplexed, Ellie glanced around and watched as Bascom deposited a pouting Priscilla into a small bench shaped like a boat that could seat two or three people.

"This boat doesn't move. You know what I wanted to ride for our maiden foyage."

Bascom winked at Ellie. Wanda's music danced around them.

"I do? Hmm." He glanced around, a frown momentarily pulling his eyebrows closer together. He snapped his fingers. "I've got it."

He walked over and swung Prissy back up into his arms, motioning Ellie to follow. Prissy began to giggle and peeked over his shoulder as if to make sure Ellie had followed his directive.

"Could it be...this?" He stopped next to matching mermaids, one slightly smaller than the other. He started to lift Priscilla onto it then stopped.

"C'mon, please?" Prissy reached forward with her leather-encased toe, her blue calico skirt draping around her out-stretched leg. "Mama, he wouldn't let me sit on here until you were here to sit on yours."

"Mine?" Ellie stepped closer, noticing for the first time that the larger beautiful creature mirrored her own features. "Oh, Bascom."

"She looks just like you, Mama! And look, mine looks like me."

Sure enough, her daughter's mermaid resembled Prissy in a most remarkable way. Long dark curls were carved in wood and decorated with paint. The younger mermaid's eyes sparkled brown, just like Prissy's.

"I'm not sure I could ever be quite this beautiful, but the coloring, down to the green eyes, and features do mimic mine in a most amazing way." She circled around the mermaid and then did the same with her daughter's. "And, Prissy, you're right. Your mermaid is the spitting image of you! She's beautiful, honey."

Prissy leaned forward and hugged her mermaid. Ellie hadn't realized the scope of Bascom's talent until now. He didn't deserve to be hidden away out here when he could receive accolades from clients all over the world.

He seemed to read her emotions and leaned close. "What brings such a forlorn expression to your face? I thought you'd like them. If you don't. . .I can replace her with something—anything—else. I didn't mean to make you uncomfortable, though you truly are every bit as beautiful—even more so—than this carved figure."

"It's not that." Ellie searched his eyes. "It's just that you have a talent I've never seen before. It doesn't seem right to hide you, or this, away."

"Who's hiding?" Bascom smiled. "I don't need an audience to create. I don't like the hoopla that comes along with the career like some do. I prefer to work and be left alone. I carve to honor the gift that God gave me. But I want the glory of the talent to go to Him, not to me."

"Let's go, let's go, let's go!" Prissy's patience had become frayed.

Bascom waited a moment more, looking into Ellie's eyes for approval. She searched his face for any sign of remorse, but only found love shining out from his eyes. She allowed her mouth to drift into a smile. "If you're sure."

"Positive." He stole a quick kiss and jumped to the center of the attraction where he placed his hand over a small handle. "Prissy, do you remember what I taught you?"

"Yes, sir. I have to hold on tight. The steam has been building for almost two hours. When you pull the lever, the steam will release and we'll begin to spin."

The last word was uttered in pure reverence at the idea. Ellie couldn't help but catch her daughter's exuberance. Bascom jumped back onto the platform and hurried to her side. Before she could move, he gently grasped her waist and lifted her to sit sideways upon her own mermaid. She clung to the bar, not sure what to expect.

"Excellent description, Prissy." He turned to Ellie. "We've primed her for weeks about the process. I can't believe she didn't tell you and that she kept the secret so well. I'm proud of that little girl."

Ellie didn't think any words could make her heart swell any bigger. Hearing the man she loved talk about her daughter's precociousness melted something deep inside.

Bascom returned to the lever. He grinned and sent Ellie a wink. Her stomach fluttered, as much from the wink as from the anticipation. He placed his work-hardened hand upon the shiny piece of metal. Prissy squealed. Slowly, he moved the lever into position and the ride began to spin, slowly at first, but gaining in momentum as the seconds passed. Ellie grasped the pole in front of her for a moment, but relaxed her hold as the ride steadied its pace.

Priscilla laughed with abandon but clutched her own pole with white-knuckled fingers. Bascom jumped aboard and stood between them.

Releasing one hand from the pole, Prissy gripped Bascom's sleeve. "Tell her about the ring."

Ellie glanced at her daughter. The room spun around them, making the gaslights blur behind her daughter's silhouette. "The ring?"

Wanda continued to play a lighthearted tune on the organ, which added a festive flair to the moment.

"The ring." Bascom wrapped one arm around Ellie's waist and pointed with his finger to the edge of the ride's canopy above them. "If you can grasp the ring, you get a free ride."

"Really." Ellie fought back her grin as she studied the small brass circle before it whisked past her head. "And if I miss?"

Bascom's deep chuckle filled the air around her. "Then I suppose you could end up in a heap on the floor."

Ellie now understood why straw had been brought in to surround the structure. She clutched the pole more tightly. "I'd rather that not happen."

She watched as Bascom edged his way around her mermaid. The carved piece of wood rode up and down as the pole moved in a similar fashion. Bascom leaned out and much to Prissy's delight, snatched the ring from its resting place.

"You did it, Mr. Bascom, you did it!" Prissy almost fell off her mermaid in excitement. Ellie clutched her arm and pushed her back into place.

Bascom jumped back to the center flooring and pushed the lever back into its original position.

Prissy cried out in dismay.

"It's okay, Priss. We have a lot of guests waiting for their turn, and you'll be able to ride to your heart's content with them. But for now, I have something special for both of you."

"Yes, sir."

Bascom helped them off their respective mounts, and they stepped from the platform. Prissy ran off to collect Wanda while Ellie's world continued to spin. Bascom kept a firm grip on her arm and led her to a nearby chair. He knelt down beside it and turned his closed fist until it faced fingers up. "I have something for you. I hope you'll accept it."

Slowly he opened his fingers, and Ellie saw a beautiful gold ring lying upon his palm. She glanced over to see the brass ring once again in place on the carousel. How he'd managed to slip it back up there and switch it out with this ring was beyond her.

"This ring will come to mean so much to both of us. It represents the circular shape of the carousel, which first brought us together. It represents my love for you and for Prissy—you've helped me come full circle from my grief to a new hope for the future. And it represents the circle of love that will flow between us and our Lord, constantly growing as we move forward in love for each other and Him."

"Oh, Bascom, that's beautiful. I do accept the ring and all that it represents." She watched as he slipped the golden band onto her right index finger. "I never dreamed my carousel would come with treasure."

"When we marry, I'll take great joy in moving the ring to your other hand."

Wanda and Prissy moved into Ellie's line of vision. Bascom eased himself back to his feet. Ellie waggled her finger at them, and they oohed and ahhed for a moment.

Bascom motioned Prissy closer. "Prissy, I have a treasure for you, too."

"Really? Where?"

He walked over to the refreshment counter and reached below to pull out a miniature replica of their carousel, but this one's lettering read differently.

"Carousel Dreams," Ellie read out loud to her daughter.

"My very own carousel?" Prissy clapped her hands together and squealed louder than she had on the ride. She leaned closer. "It even has the Mama and Prissy mermaids."

She turned, and without warning, threw herself into Bascom's embrace. "I love it. And I love you. Thank you!" Tears ran down the little girl's face.

"You're welcome." Bascom, his voice choked up, lifted her high into his arms where she buried her face in his shoulder. "And I love you, too."

Ellie raised her hand to her mouth and watched both through tear-blurred eyes. She caressed her new ring with her thumb as a secret smile moved across her face. Only one more event would supersede the preciousness of the moment, and that special day would soon come.

epilogue

"Mama." Priscilla's voice dropped to a childish whisper of awe. "You're so pretty! You look like the Princess of Whimsy."

Ellie smiled and adjusted her skirts, bending her knees so she could lower to her daughter's level. She balanced on the balls of her feet and whispered back. "No, *you* look like the Princess of Whimsy. Just look at you in that beautiful gown. I'm so proud of you, sweetheart."

Priscilla's gaze grew solemn. "Are we really going to marry Bascom now?"

Ellie could hear Wanda's chuckle from where she stood across the small room. She exchanged a happy smile with her friend. "We really are."

"I like him."

"So do I. He's going to make us very happy."

"We'll make him happy, too, Mama. Remember how sad he was when he came here?"

"I do." Ellie thought back to the day of his arrival. Though deep down her heart instantly recognized her future husband, her mind and rationality had rebelled. She couldn't see past her grandfather's foolish notion to build the carousel, and still reeling from grief over his death, had lashed out at Bascom unfairly. "But now he's happy again. He's getting a new wife and a wonderful daughter."

"That he is," Wanda agreed, coming over to help Ellie up. "And you're going to sweep him off his feet when he sees you. But only if you stop talking and get out there for the ceremony."

"I thought I was the one who was supposed to be swept off

my feet," Ellie teased. The sound of voices from outside carried through the wall, and Ellie tried to quell the butterflies that danced inside her stomach. She knew without a doubt that marrying Bascom would bring them all a lot of joy. Things had certainly changed during the past two months.

"And I'm guessing he will. I saw him a bit earlier, and he's heart-stopping handsome in his suit. I saw every woman in the room stop talking and stare after his arrival. You've got a good man there, Ellie, and you'd best hurry out and snatch him up."

"He is a good man. I wish it hadn't taken me so long to realize it."

"I think you both realized it from that first moment in the parlor. Or at least everyone around you did. Your grandmother asked me to begin work on your dress that very night."

Ellie laughed. "Now you're teasing me."

"I'm not!" Wanda faked her indignation, lightening the mood for them both. "She pulled me aside and said, 'My granddaughter has just met her match. If my intuition is correct, you need to start work on a wedding dress for her and fast!'"

Mortified, Ellie laughed. "It was that obvious?"

"To all of us, yes. To the two of you, apparently not. I think Sheldon saw it, too, which is why he started in on his new vendetta so quickly—a plan that failed miserably. But you two, you're both so stubborn it took some time to get past your defenses and see that you'd each met your perfect match."

Ellie took a deep breath and checked her appearance once more in the looking glass. She'd pinned her dark hair up on top of her head, but tendrils had drifted down to frame her square face. Not wanting to take time to set the wayward pieces to right, she ignored them. She smiled at Wanda. "Well, then, if you think I'm ready, I'd like to go get hitched."

"You're radiant." Wanda's tear-filled eyes met hers in the

reflection. "The dress couldn't fit better, both for you and the occasion."

The full skirt of the white dress brushed the ground. Small white shell-shaped appliqués pulled the sheer top layer's hem up at intervals, holding it in place about a foot above the under layer's hem. The neck scooped down gracefully, finished with tatting also in the shape of shells, and simple long sleeves hugged her arms. The bodice clung tightly and tapered to her waist, where the fabric flared out into the full skirt.

"It does look wonderful," Ellie agreed. "And I have you to thank for that. I had no idea you'd create such an elegant gown. How did you ever come up with the idea?"

"I've only listened to your Whimsy tales for how long? The dress lived in your imagination long before I ever put it to fabric. You might convince yourself that your stories are for Prissy, but I know they really come from your heart. A princess wedding will only be complete if there's a princess. . .or two."

They both looked at Priscilla where she stood on tiptoe, peering out the window toward the festivities. Her daughter, frothed in layers of girlie pastel pink, indeed looked her part. They laughed at her continuous narration of the events unfolding outside their window. "Oh, there's a carriage with the reverend. And his wife is carrying a platter of food. I wonder what they have. I'm hungry—can we eat soon? Will we have Whimsy tale food? What do they eat in Whimsy?"

She didn't seem to notice her mother's and housekeeper's lack of response; she just continued to watch and review.

"I'm ready, Wanda." Ellie hugged her friend and turned to her daughter. "Come along. Shall we go see exactly what will happen in the land of Whimsy on this day?"

Prissy grabbed her hand and led the way outdoors. The sky was clear with no cloud in sight. Blue stretched before them and disappeared over the rooftop of the pavilion. They strolled slowly in the direction of what had become known as the event of the year. Ellie smiled up at the sign that hung low over the pavilion's door frame. It matched the name on Prissy's new toy.

CAROUSEL DREAMS.

She hoped all those who entered would find a way to reach their own personal dreams. She had every one of hers she could imagine. Good friends, a good life, her daughter, and soon, her husband.

The last few stragglers hurried inside at her appearance. Ellie stopped at the door and waited for Wanda to step ahead. After a few deep breaths to calm her racing pulse, she stepped through the open doorway.

Again, awe and disbelief stopped her just inside, reminiscent of Bascom's first unveiling a few short weeks earlier. He'd formed the entry into a shop of sorts, and small carousels—miniatures of the ones he'd carved on the main attraction itself—lined the shelves. Candies in jars and other small trinkets also lined the counters. The effect was that of a small fair, right inside their pavilion. The carousel embodied the several Whimsy tale characters that Ellie had spoken of—a fish, a dolphin, and a seahorse along with standard horses. The outside edges of the structure, both top and platform, were carved into the shape of waves and rimmed with seashells. The centerpieces, Ellie's favorite part, were the matching mother and daughter mermaids, carved to match her and Prissy's features.

When she'd first seen them, she couldn't stop the smile that filled her face. Bascom, with his unique talent and ability, had captured her imaginary world and corralled it into reality. She knew he must have stayed up late into the night, on many occasions, to get the details honed to match her stories in so little time.

She mourned the talent Sheldon had also brought to the attraction and prayed for him often. She hoped he'd someday lose the bitterness, turn his life over to God, and find joy in living free from the previous burdens.

But today the room had been transformed even more into a fairy-tale setting; sheer fabrics and ribbon and greenery draped from every ceiling fixture available. Expectant faces watched to see the bride's expression. Prissy's warm hand tightened around Ellie's. For once, her daughter was speechless.

And now Ellie, though she'd taken a moment to observe the beauty and breathtaking scene before her, had eyes for only one man. She felt as if she were walking on air as she floated on happiness and stopped before him.

His expression matched her feeling of awe as he drank in the sight of her in the princess dress. "You're so beautiful." His whisper mimicked Priscilla's earlier response to the dress, and tears formed in Ellie's eyes at the display of love reflecting back from his.

"Thank you." She reveled in his presence. He'd dressed the part of a handsome prince. A long black swallowtail coat hugged his slender torso while a deep blue vest that perfectly matched the color of his eyes glistened in shiny fabric from beneath. The top of a pleated white shirt peeked out above the vest, complete with a black silk cravat tied neatly beneath his collar. Slim dark Edgewood pants with tiny blue and white pinstripes completed the ensemble. The style matched Ellie's dress and their Whimsy theme perfectly.

But her handsome prince himself took her breath away. Thick wavy locks of sun-kissed brown hair neatly brushed across his forehead and flipped back over his ears from a side part. His blue eyes twinkled with life, giving the suggestion of an unspoken joke that waited to spill from his lips. And those lips. . .they curved up to the left and highlighted the dimple in his cheek. His whole appearance shone with happiness. The burdens he'd arrived with were left behind, and the new man before her exuded a calm exuberance.

"Where've you been?" His words were low, for her ears only.

Perplexed, Ellie glanced out the window. "In the house."

He laughed. "All my life?"

"Well, no." She laughed back. "But I've been waiting right here."

"I'm glad you waited."

"Me, too." She leaned closer. "And I'm glad you found me."

"Me, too," he echoed. He closed his eyes and leaned his forehead against hers.

Ellie could feel his soft breath against her face and savored the closeness. Bascom opened his eyes, captured her hand in his, and brought it to his lips for a gentle kiss. Their audience oohed and ahhed around them.

"You're blushing, Ellie."

He didn't have to tell her that. She'd forgotten about their guests; so absorbed was she in his presence that they'd melted into the background. But at their enthusiastic murmurings, she quickly remembered they weren't alone. The pastor saved her from the moment.

He called them all together and asked them to circle around Ellie and Bascom. Ellie distracted herself from further thoughts of her future husband by looking around to see who had come to help them celebrate this most special of days. All her closest neighbors were there, as well as a lot of friends from town. The celebration carried more meaning for those nearby, who could also celebrate the fact that the vandalism had been thwarted and the villain placed behind bars.

She saw guests from the resort and friends of Bascom's that had come from afar, even on such short notice. They'd arrived during the past few days and had filled her resort and several others around them. She also saw a few reporters.

"Why do the men over there have cameras? They look too official to be guests."

Bascom followed her gaze. "They're friends from back East. They caught the train in when they heard about Sheldon and the wedding."

He caressed her hand and leaned close to speak into her ear. "They'd followed the story back in Coney and tried hard to find a witness or anyone who could help shed some light on what happened. When they couldn't, they felt they'd let me down. Those men followed my entire career and were devastated, almost as much as me, when things fell apart. I felt it only right to let them know things had come to a close in that area of my life and also to know that a new chapter was about to begin."

"They're doing a story on our wedding?"

"The wedding, the attacks, and Carousel Dreams. We'll get a lot of publicity from this. I'll promote your books. . ."

"Which aren't even written on paper yet."

"But it's never too early to start the publicity."

"Always thinking ahead, aren't you?" Ellie realized her husband-to-be had a lot of facets to him that she'd never examined. She knew it would take years to examine them all—and she savored the thought.

"You're going to be a success, Ellie. I'll make sure of it. You'll never worry again about the resort or money or being alone. Not if I can help it."

"Judging by the crowd around your figurines, we won't have to worry anyway."

"I know." Bascom frowned. "They're getting more attention at the moment than our wedding. And you, my princess, deserve to be the center of attention—not the wood carvings. We need to do something about that."

Before she could say another word, he spun her around until her back pressed against his chest and she faced their guests. He wrapped his arms securely around her waist and snuggled his head against hers. She clutched his hands with hers. Never one to like being the center of attention, she clung to his solid strength. "I'd like to thank you all for coming to see this fairy-tale wedding between my beautiful bride and myself. If you all don't mind, we'd like to get the process started so we can begin our life together."

Everyone laughed and the crowd moved closer. Prissy pushed her way through, and Bascom leaned down to peek around and smile at Ellie. "Are you ready?"

"More than." She'd never been so sure of anything in her life.

With Priscilla's hand clutching one of hers and her other securely tucked under Bascom's steady arm, Ellie turned to face the pastor. In her eagerness she had to force her feet to stay flat on the floor. Like Prissy, bobbing up and down beside her, Ellie wanted to bounce the ceremony away.

The words drifted past in a blur, and finally Ellie heard the words she'd been eagerly awaiting. "I now pronounce you man and wife. You may kiss the bride."

Prissy's distraction of the guests was perfectly timed as she squealed with joy and clapped her hands.

Ellie took advantage of the moment, entwined her hands in Bascom's lapels, and gently tugged him forward. She grinned at his expression of surprise. She had a few facets for him to learn about, too. "Kiss me, Bascom Anthony."

Bascom leaned closer. "Yes'm, I believe I will."

A Letter To Our Readers

Dear Reader:

In order that we might better contribute to your reading enjoyment, we would appreciate your taking a few minutes to respond to the following questions. We welcome your comments and read each form and letter we receive. When completed, please return to the following:

Fiction Editor
Heartsong Presents
PO Box 719
Uhrichsville, Ohio 44683

1. Did you enjoy reading *Carousel Dreams* by Paige Winship Dooly?

   ❏ Very much! I would like to see more books by this author!

   ❏ Moderately. I would have enjoyed it more if

   _____

   _____

   _____

2. Are you a member of **Heartsong Presents**? ❏ Yes ❏ No

   If no, where did you purchase this book? _____

   _____

3. How would you rate, on a scale from 1 (poor) to 5 (superior), the cover design? _____

4. On a scale from 1 (poor) to 10 (superior), please rate the following elements.

   ____ Heroine   ____ Plot

   ____ Hero   ____ Inspirational theme

   ____ Setting   ____ Secondary characters

5. These characters were special because? _____

_____

_____

6. How has this book inspired your life?_____

_____

_____

7. What settings would you like to see covered in future
   Heartsong Presents books? _____

_____

_____

8. What are some inspirational themes you would like to see
   treated in future books? _____

_____

_____

9. Would you be interested in reading other **Heartsong
   Presents** titles? ❏ Yes ❏ No

10. Please check your age range:

    ❏ Under 18   ❏ 18-24
    ❏ 25-34   ❏ 35-45
    ❏ 46-55   ❏ Over 55

Name _____

Occupation _____

Address _____

City, State, Zip_____

Heart♥ng

Any 12
Heartsong
Presents titles
for only
$27.00*

HISTORICAL ROMANCE IS CHEAPER BY THE DOZEN!

Buy any assortment of twelve *Heartsong Presents* titles and save 25% off of the already discounted price of $2.97 each!

*plus $4.00 shipping and handling per order and sales tax where applicable.
If outside the U.S. please call 740-922-7280 for shipping charges.

HEARTSONG PRESENTS TITLES AVAILABLE NOW:

(If ordering from this page, please remember to include it with the order form.)

Presents

___HP716 *Spinning Out of Control,*
         V. McDonough
___HP719 *Weaving a Future,* S. P. Davis
___HP720 *Bridge Across the Sea,* P. Griffin
___HP723 *Adam's Bride,* L. Harris
___HP724 *A Daughter's Quest,* L. N. Dooley
___HP727 *Wyoming Hoofbeats,* S. P. Davis
___HP728 *A Place of Her Own,* L. A. Coleman
___HP731 *The Bounty Hunter and the Bride,*
         V. McDonough
___HP732 *Lonely in Longtree,* J. Stengl
___HP735 *Deborah,* M. Colvin
___HP736 *A Time to Plant,* K. E. Hake
___HP740 *The Castaway's Bride,* S. P. Davis
___HP741 *Golden Dawn,* C. M. Hake
___HP743 *Broken Bow,* I. Brand
___HP744 *Golden Days,* M. Connealy
___HP747 *A Wealth Beyond Riches,*
         V. McDonough
___HP748 *Golden Twilight,* K. Y'Barbo
___HP751 *The Music of Home,* T. H. Murray
___HP752 *Tara's Gold,* L. Harris
___HP755 *Journey to Love,* L. Bliss
___HP756 *The Lumberjack's Lady,* S. P. Davis
___HP759 *Stirring Up Romance,* J. L. Barton
___HP760 *Mountains Stand Strong,* I. Brand
___HP763 *A Time to Keep,* K. E. Hake

___HP764 *To Trust an Outlaw,* R. Gibson
___HP767 *A Bride Idea,* Y. Lehman
___HP768 *Sharon Takes a Hand,* R. Dow
___HP771 *Canteen Dreams,* C. Putman
___HP772 *Corduroy Road to Love,* L. A. Coleman
___HP775 *Treasure in the Hills,* P. W. Dooly
___HP776 *Betsy's Return,* W. E. Brunstetter
___HP779 *Joanna's Adventure,* M. J. Conner
___HP780 *The Dreams of Hannah Williams,*
         L. Ford
___HP783 *Seneca Shadows,* L. Bliss
___HP784 *Promises, Promises,* A. Miller
___HP787 *A Time to Laugh,* K. Hake
___HP788 *Uncertain Alliance,* M. Davis
___HP791 *Better Than Gold,* L. A. Eakes
___HP792 *Sweet Forever,* R. Cecil
___HP795 *A Treasure Reborn,* P. Griffin
___HP796 *The Captain's Wife,* M. Davis
___HP799 *Sandhill Dreams,* C. C. Putman
___HP800 *Return to Love,* S. P. Davis
___HP803 *Quills and Promises,* A. Miller
___HP804 *Reckless Rogue,* M. Davis
___HP811 *A New Joy,* S. P. Davis
___HP812 *Everlasting Promise,* R. K. Cecil
___HP815 *A Treasure Regained,* P. Griffin
___HP816 *Wild at Heart,* V. McDonough

Great Inspirational Romance at a Great Price!

Heartsong Presents books are inspirational romances in contemporary and historical settings, designed to give you an enjoyable, spirit-lifting reading experience. You can choose wonderfully written titles from some of today's best authors like Wanda E. Brunstetter, Mary Connealy, Susan Page Davis, Cathy Marie Hake, Joyce Livingston, and many others.

When ordering quantities less than twelve, above titles are $2.97 each.
Not all titles may be available at time of order.